Growing Up with Aloha

A Nanea Classic
Volume 1

by Kirby Larson

★ American Girl®

Published by American Girl Publishing

17 18 19 20 21 22 23 LEO 10 9 8 7 6 5 4 3 2 1

All American Girl marks, BeForever™, Nanea™, and Nanea Mitchell™ are
trademarks of American Girl.

"Mai Poina 'Oe Ia'u" composed by Lizzie Doiron

This book is a work of fiction. Any similarity to real persons, living or dead, is
coincidental and not intended by American Girl. References to real events, people,
or places are used fictitiously. Other names, characters, places, and incidents are the
products of imagination.

Cover image by David Roth and Juliana Kolesova
Author photo by Meryl Schenker
Grateful acknowledgement is made to the following for permission to use images in
the cover design: Photograph/advertisement of "Aloha to the Lurline . . . And You"
is used under license from Matson Navigation Company, Inc.; "Waikiki Beach"
© iStock.com/delamofoto; "Splash" © iStock.com/ShaneMyersPhoto; "Frangipanis
Flowers" © iStock.com/JulienGrondin.

Cataloging-in-Publication Data available from the Library of Congress

For Clio, my mo'opuna wahine, with much aloha

Beforever™

The adventurous characters you'll meet in
the BeForever books will spark your curiosity
about the past, inspire you to find your voice
in the present, and excite you about your future.
You'll make friends with these girls as you share
their fun and their challenges. Like you, they are
bright and brave, imaginative and energetic,
creative and kind. Just as you are, they are
discovering what really matters: Helping others.
Being a true friend. Protecting the earth.
Standing up for what's right. Read their stories,
explore their worlds, join their adventures.
Your friendship with them will BeForever.

❀ TABLE *of* CONTENTS ❀

Nanea lives in Hawaii on the island of Oahu, so you'll see some Hawaiian words in this book. The meaning and pronunciation of these words are provided in the glossary on page 202.

Nanea's name is pronounced *nah-NAY-ah*. It means "delightful and pleasant."

NOT THE BABY OF THE FAMILY

S unlight slivered through the blinds. Nanea Mitchell stretched, breathing in the sweet outside smells of ginger and plumeria and the savory inside smells of breakfast. Sausage! *Mele* thumped her tail in anticipation.

"Good morning, you silly *poi* dog," Nanea said, giving Mele a pat. She hopped out of bed and turned the wall calendar from October to November 1941. It was Saturday, so Nanea put on a sleeveless blouse printed with tiki huts and palm trees and a pair of white shorts.

Her fifteen-year-old sister, Mary Lou, yawned, loosening her braids as she slid out of her bed across the room. She walked to the vanity, shaking her dark waves over her shoulders, and clicked on her little Admiral radio.

"Your hair looks nice," Nanea said.

Mary Lou picked up her hairbrush and turned to Nanea. "Let me fix yours."

"It's fine!" Nanea leaped out of reach.

"Alice Nanea Mitchell!" Mary Lou scolded, using Nanea's full name. Papa had picked Alice, which was Grandmom Mitchell's name, and Mom had picked Nanea, which meant "delightful and pleasant." "Sometimes you are so childish," Mary Lou sighed.

"Not today." Nanea picked up her *'eke hula*, a basket for carrying costumes and implements. "See? I'm all ready for hula class."

While Mary Lou got dressed, Nanea made sure she had both sets of wooden dancing sticks. The *kala'au* were the size of a ruler; when she hit them together, they made a *tick-tick* sound like the big clock in her third-grade classroom. The longer *pu'ili* made a happy noise that reminded Nanea of the cash register at Pono's Market, her grandparents' store.

That reminded her of something else. "Why can't I go to work with you after class today?" she asked. "*Tutu* says I'm a big help."

"Tutu spoils you," Mary Lou answered, fluffing her

hair, "because you're the baby of the family."

Nanea knew that their grandmother did *not* spoil her, and that she was *not* a baby. But before she could say anything to Mary Lou, "Chattanooga Choo-Choo" came on the radio. Mary Lou grabbed Nanea's hands and twirled her around the room, singing along with the radio.

When the song ended, Mary Lou said, "Gosh, that was fun." Her eyes sparkled.

"Hula is prettier." Nanea made the motion for swimming fish.

Tail wagging, Mele licked Nanea's hands.

Nanea laughed. "These aren't real fish, you goofy dog!"

"What's going on in here?" David asked as he ducked his head into the girls' bedroom, sending in a wave of Old Spice aftershave.

Nanea noticed the ukulele case in his hand. "You playing today?" she asked.

Seventeen-year-old David worked as a bellboy at the Royal Hawaiian Hotel, but sometimes he filled in when one of the other musicians was sick, or surfing.

"Maybe," he said. "I'm a Boy Scout. I'm always prepared." When her big brother smiled, Nanea thought he was as handsome as any movie star. "Breakfast is ready. Come on."

The girls followed him to the kitchen.

"Good morning!" Nanea said, kissing Papa's cheek. His hair was wet from the shower.

"More like good night for me," Papa replied. He worked the graveyard shift, so he went to bed after breakfast, which was really his dinner. "Do you like my aftershave?" Papa grinned. "Instead of Old Spice, it's Old Fuel."

Nanea had heard that joke a million times, but she laughed anyway. Nothing washed away the smell of oil that Papa got from working as a welder at the Pearl Harbor shipyard. There were so many ships. And planes, too, at Hickam Air Field next to the shipyard. David said because Pearl Harbor was a big deal in the Pacific, Papa was a big deal in the Pacific. That always made Papa laugh.

Nanea turned to her mother. "Why can't I work at Pono's Market? I'm nearly ten."

Mom tucked a stray lock of hair behind Nanea's

ear. "Don't be in such a hurry to grow up."

"Yeah, Monkey." David waved his fork. "Enjoy being a kid as long as you can."

"I would love to be nine again," Mary Lou said. "No responsibilities."

Nanea frowned. She had plenty of responsibilities! She took care of Mele and set the table and always turned in her homework on time. But Nanea wanted grown-up responsibilities, like working at the market.

"Is that a storm cloud on someone's face?" Papa teased Nanea.

She leaned her head against her father's. His hair was carrot-red and hers was black; he had blue eyes, she had hazel. The Mitchell kids were all born on Oahu like Mom. Papa had been born in Beaverton, Oregon, far away. He grew up on a farm, not in a city like Honolulu. Despite those differences, Nanea and Papa were very much alike. They loved many of the same things: the funnies, fishing, and dogs—especially Mele. Nanea wrapped her arms around Papa's neck and squeezed two times. That was their secret code for "Buddies forever."

She sat down and poured a glass of fresh pineapple

juice. "Being the youngest doesn't mean I can't do grown-up things," Nanea complained. She wondered why her *'ohana*, her family, never gave her the chance to prove it.

Papa smiled. "I remember chomping at the bit to drive the tractor on Grandpop Mitchell's farm. It was so hard to wait until I was thirteen."

"And your grandfather said I had to learn the times tables before I could run the cash register." Mom poured herself more coffee. "It took a lot of flash cards before I rang up that first sale."

"*Tutu Kane* said you were nine," Nanea said. "My age."

Papa pretended to cast a line. "I hear the fish are biting," he said. "Maybe later, you could round up the other two Kittens to catch us some supper." He called Nanea and her two best friends, Lily Suda and Donna Hill, the Three Kittens after the nursery rhyme.

"Today I want to help," Nanea pouted, "more than I want to fish."

At the sound of her favorite word, Mele barked.

"I agree, Mele. Some fresh fish would be so *'ono*, delicious." Papa waggled his eyebrows, and Nanea had to laugh. When Papa said Hawaiian words, he sounded like a newcomer even though he'd lived on Oahu for years.

"Look at the time!" Mom handed Nanea some warm guava bread. "This is for your grandparents. Now you girls better scoot!"

Outside, Mary Lou's rubber slippers slapped against the sidewalk while Nanea's bare feet made soft *pat-pat-pat* sounds. Mele ran behind them. She had come to hula lessons since the day Nanea had started when she was four years old. Tutu didn't mind. She said Mele's wagging tail meant that she didn't have to sweep the linoleum!

At Tutu's, Nanea and Mary Lou joined the other dancers lined up outside the *lanai*. The covered porch at the back of the house was Tutu's hula studio.

When Tutu pulled out the *ipu*, gourd drum, everyone quieted. Nanea gathered her thoughts, focusing her heart and her mind on the lesson to come.

"*Makaukau?*" Tutu began every class by asking the dancers if they were ready.

"*Ae,*" the girls answered. Yes.

With Tutu marking time on the ipu, the dancers

warmed up by practicing all their basic hula steps.

"Very nice," Tutu said. She set the drum aside and put a record on the phonograph. As "Lovely Hula Hands" began to play, the dancers Nanea's age formed their lines and began their hula. Then they moved on to "My Yellow Ginger Lei." Such *hapa haole* songs, which combined English words with Hawaiian melodies, always brought smiles to the tourists' faces. They were also popular with the soldiers who came to the United Service Organization programs. Tutu's students had been regular USO performers for many years.

Mary Lou's group of older girls danced to songs that used both Hawaiian words and melodies. Maybe someday Nanea would be good enough to dance a solo, like the one Mary Lou was practicing. Nanea thought her sister was doing the steps perfectly, but in the middle of the song, Tutu lifted the needle from the record.

"Noelani," she began, calling Mary Lou by her Hawaiian middle name, "you must remember to keep your fingers soft and your back straight." Tutu had been dancing since she was a little girl, so it was easy for her to demonstrate what she meant.

As she placed the needle back on the record, Tutu spoke to all the dancers. "There is no shame in a mistake. There is only shame in not learning from it."

Tutu's corrections never sounded like scoldings. She was a *kumu hula*, a master teacher who had been teaching for many years, just as her mother taught before her.

Nanea held her head high, honored to carry on the hula tradition that had been part of her family for generations.

🌺

After class, Nanea and Mary Lou sat on the front porch with Tutu enjoying Mom's guava bread. It wasn't long before David arrived to give Tutu and Mary Lou a ride to Pono's Market. Mary Lou picked up her 'eke hula. "See you later, sis," she said.

Tutu brushed crumbs from the skirt of her *mu'umu'u* and gave Nanea a kiss good-bye. "*Aloha, keiki,*" she said. "You did well in class today."

Nanea watched Mary Lou climb into the backseat while David held the passenger door open for Tutu. With a wave, David drove off, and Nanea turned and headed the other way, toward home.

If only Nanea was going to the store, too! She would sort all the penny candy into the right jars while Tutu Kane talked with the customers. Nanea would tidy the colorful displays of produce and dust the shelves of canned goods. She would straighten the bolts of fabric without even being asked. And she'd open the doors for the neighborhood aunties—the older women she'd known her whole life—as they left with their shopping bags bulging with purchases that Tutu had rung up. "Mary Lou would see I'm not a baby anymore," Nanea told Mele as they walked home. "If only I could help."

Mele wagged her tail in agreement.

Nanea wasn't surprised to find a peanut butter sandwich waiting for her at home. But she was surprised when Mom asked for help with the ironing.

Finally, a grown-up job!

But Mom hadn't meant for Nanea to use the hot iron. Nanea was to sprinkle the dry, starched clothes with water, then roll them into hot dog shapes so Mom could press out the wrinkles later. Another baby job.

Nanea was sprinkling Papa's last work shirt when there was a knock at the door. *A-roo! Aroo!* Mele sang her greeting. Her name meant "song."

"*Komo mai*, welcome!" Nanea called to the other two Kittens. "Or should I say, *Komo meow*?"

Lily Suda made a small bow. She was Nanea's oldest friend, and the Mitchells and Sudas were like family. Nanea called Lily's parents Uncle Fudge and Aunt Betty, and Lily called Nanea's parents Uncle Richard and Aunt May. The families lived on the same street, shared meals, and celebrated holidays together. Nanea and Lily had gone out many times with Uncle Fudge on his sampan, a Japanese fishing boat, to help him catch *'ahi* and other fish to sell. Aunt Betty taught the girls how to fold origami geckos and koi and cranes.

That was one of the best things about living in Hawaii. The islands were like a jigsaw puzzle where people of all different shapes and colors fit together. There were people from Japan, like Aunt Betty and Uncle Fudge, and from Portugal, like their mailman Mr. Cruz, and from China, like Mrs. Lin who had a tiny crack seed shop where she sold dried fruits. And of course there were haoles, like Papa, and Donna's family, who came from all over the mainland.

Behind Lily, Donna chomped on her bubble gum. Donna's family had moved from San Francisco three years earlier so her father could work in the Pearl Harbor shipyard, like Papa. Donna had walked up to Nanea and Lily in first grade and said, "Hi! What are your names?" After school, Donna had given them each a piece of bubble gum, and that was the beginning of the Three Kittens.

When her family first arrived in Honolulu, Donna had been reluctant to try any new foods. But she soon learned to love Aunt Betty's sweet rice *mochi*, Portuguese *malasada* doughnuts, and especially Mom's guava bread.

Now Donna stopped chewing her gum. "Do I smell guava bread?" she asked.

Mom laughed. "I baked two loaves in case some hungry Kittens wandered by." She cut three thick slices while Donna disposed of her gum.

The girls took the bread out on the porch so that they wouldn't wake Nanea's father, who was still sleeping. Mele kicked up puffs of red dust as she paced, begging for bites.

"How was hula class?" Lily asked. She couldn't take

Saturday morning lessons with Tutu because that's when she had Japanese language class. But Lily liked dancing as much as Nanea did. Donna had tried taking hula lessons, but she decided she wasn't much of a dancer.

"It was fun," Nanea answered. "Tutu started to teach us a new dance to perform at the USO Christmas show next month." Then Nanea looked at Donna. "What do you have there?"

"Take a look." Donna lifted her arm and the newspaper slid out.

Nanea caught it before it fell in the dirt. "Isn't this your dad's?" Nanea had never met anyone who was so interested in the news. Mr. Hill was always talking to Papa about the war in Europe.

Donna took another bite of bread. "He saw something we'd be interested in."

"What?" Lily asked.

Donna shrugged. "He said we'd find it."

Nanea opened the paper, skimming headlines about battles in Germany and Russia.

"It seems like everybody's in the war except America," Lily said.

"Skip those war stories," Donna said. "They don't have anything to do with us here on Oahu."

Nanea pressed her finger to the paper. "A contest!"

"The Honolulu Helping Hands Contest," read Lily. "Sounds nifty."

"That must be what Dad meant," Donna said.

"The grand prize is a brand new Schwinn bike," Nanea added.

Donna whistled. "That *is* interesting."

"What are the rules?" Lily asked.

"We have to do these four things by December fifteenth to win the bike," Nanea explained, pointing to the list.

"*Enter* to win, you mean," said Lily.

Donna counted on her fingers. "That's a month and a half from now. We'd have to check off one thing about every two weeks."

Lily leaned over Nanea's shoulder. "The first one's a snap: Do a good deed for a stranger. But look at the second one: Show appreciation for your family." She made a face. "That means I'd have to do something nice for Tommy." Even Nanea had to admit that Lily's little brother was a handful.

"How can a kid make a difference in the community?" Donna asked, reading the third requirement.

"What about that last task: Turn trouble into triumph?" Lily said. "I don't know what that means."

"Maybe it's like finding the silver lining?" Nanea suggested. One of her troubles was that her family always treated her like a baby. Where was the silver lining in that?

Donna shook her head. "This seems too hard."

"I agree," Lily said. "Even if you did everything, you might not win the bike."

Nanea pictured herself looking so grown-up on a shiny new bike. *Wait a minute!* Nanea thought, jumping up. *Doing everything for the contest and winning that bike would surely prove that she wasn't a baby!*

"I'll be right back." Nanea ran inside, quickly returning with a piece of paper and a pencil.

"What are you doing?" Lily asked.

"I'm copying down the rules." Nanea smiled. "I'm going to enter this contest. And I'm going to win!"

KOKUA

iss Smith leaned forward in her chair. "Queen Liliuokalani was Hawaii's last queen, and she was forced to give up her throne."

Nanea had heard this story many times, but her teacher was telling it in a way that made her want to listen again.

"When did this happen?" Miss Smith quizzed.

Around the room, arms flew up, including Nanea's.

"Yes, Lily?"

Lily sat up tall as she recited, "1893. January seventeenth."

Nanea knew that way back then, the rich sugar plantation owners decided they would make better rulers than the queen. They made a plan to take over the government. But those men didn't care about the

Hawaiian people the way the royal family did. It had been a long, long time since Hawaii had been ruled by royalty, but Nanea felt proud that her school—Lunalilo—was named after one of its kings.

"The queen never stopped loving these islands," explained Miss Smith. "She was a wonderful musician who wrote many songs about her homeland and people to celebrate the history and culture of Hawaii. When she died in 1917, she left all her money to the Children's Trust to help children, especially orphans." Miss Smith glanced at the classroom clock. "Oh, dear. This has been so interesting, I lost track of time. Nanea, could you please come up and write tomorrow's date on the chalkboard before the dismissal bell rings?"

Nanea hurried to the front and in her best penmanship wrote November 12, 1941. As she stared at the chalkboard, she thought about how much she loved third grade. She loved the smell of the wood shavings when she sharpened her pencil at the shiny red sharpener on the wall. She loved the spinning globe and the pull-down maps and the way Miss Smith made learning fun with math bees and read-alouds. *Maybe someday I could be a teacher, too!* Nanea thought.

"Quit daydreaming!" Donna grabbed Nanea's hand after the bell sounded. "We don't want to be late!"

"Yeah," said Lily. "After we make *leis*, we're going to the pier for Boat Day!"

The Kittens retrieved their shoes from the cloakroom. They dashed to their neighborhood, past Nanea's house, to the cottage next door.

Rose Momi had been Nanea's neighbor for so long that she was part of Nanea's 'ohana. Nanea called her Auntie Rose. So did Lily and Donna.

Today Auntie Rose was on her back porch, surrounded by baskets of plumeria blossoms. She made beautiful leis, which she sold to the tourists on the pier. "Aloha, keiki," Auntie Rose said as the Three Kittens walked into her yard.

Nanea had made plenty of leis as part of hula class, but Donna hadn't. Auntie Rose had offered to teach her, and Lily and Nanea wanted to sit in on the lesson.

Auntie Rose gave them each a basket of flowers, along with needles and crochet thread.

"I'm all thumbs when it comes to sewing," Donna confessed, already tangled up in her length of thread.

Nanea helped Donna unwind the line and thread

her needle. "Now, dip this in the petroleum jelly," she suggested. "That keeps the blossoms from tearing."

Donna dipped her needle and then poked it at a flower petal.

"Slide your needle through the eye of the bloom," Auntie Rose told her. She showed Donna what to do. As they all worked, Auntie Rose told them what it was like to grow up on Oahu when she was a girl and how she learned to make leis from her tutu.

"One of my favorite things about Hawaii is that people take time to talk," Donna said.

"We've all grown up talking story," Nanea said. Lily nodded in agreement.

"Our ancestors didn't write down their stories," Auntie Rose explained. "They told them to one another. Talking story keeps our past alive. And taking time to talk story helps us get to really know one another. It helps us really care about our friends and neighbors."

"Well, I like it," Donna said. "When I'm your age, Auntie Rose, I'm going to talk story to my children and grandchildren about living in Honolulu." She held up her tattered lei. "But I might skip the part about how bad I am at doing *this!*"

Auntie Rose chuckled and made a few tweaks to Donna's lei. "Better?" she asked.

Donna snapped her gum happily. "Better!" she said.

When the leis were long enough, the girls tied knots and snipped off the ends. The girls modeled their creations, and Auntie Rose complimented each one, pronouncing them all *nani*, beautiful. "There is a lot of aloha, a lot of love, in these leis," she said.

Donna giggled. "Maybe aloha makes up for the lumps."

"It's time for me to get to the pier and get ready for business," Auntie Rose said.

"We need to go, too," Lily said. "My dad is giving us a ride!"

The girls showered Auntie Rose with thank-yous and then hurried up the street to Lily's house. Soon they were bouncing along in Uncle Fudge's truck. The fresh air blew Nanea's hair all around. As they got closer to the pier, she saw the Aloha Tower, the famous lighthouse that welcomed everyone into Honolulu Harbor.

Soon, Uncle Fudge eased into a parking spot, and the girls clambered out of the truck. Nanea had never been to Boat Day without her parents. She felt quite grown-up walking with her friends down Bishop and Fort Streets.

As they all thumped up the two flights of stairs to the pier, Nanea smiled at the shower of paper streamers and confetti floating down from the ship's decks. She watched island boys diving for the coins that tourists tossed into the water as the Royal Hawaiian Band played.

There were so many flowers, and the assorted aromas—plumeria, carnations, jasmine—drizzled over the crowd like syrups over shave ice. Nanea could almost taste them. Drifting above the good smells were the cries of the lei sellers: "Carnation lei fifty cents; plumeria three for a dollar!" They displayed their wares to the hundreds of tourists leaving the island for the five-day return trip to San Francisco.

Men in dark suits bought leis for women in bright print dresses, or for boys in navy poplin shorts, or for girls wearing swirling cotton skirts. Some people bought leis to keep as souvenirs. But tradition said if you offered your lei to the ocean, and it made it back to shore, you would return to the island someday. The harbor was thick with floating flowers, because anyone who had ever been to Oahu wanted to come back.

"There's Auntie Rose!" Nanea exclaimed, noticing the long line of tourists waiting to buy leis from her neighbor.

A woman with two children waited at the very end of the line. The little girl held on to her mother's skirt. The boy wore a cowboy hat and spun a lasso, trying to catch something. Nanea laughed.

The Matson liner blew its horn, signaling that it was time to board.

"I'm sorry, children," the mother said sadly. "We don't have time to buy leis after all." She took their hands, and they started for the gangplank. The kids looked so disappointed—especially the little girl.

Nanea fingered the lei around her neck. She made a decision. "Wait!" she called, running after the family. Lily and Donna ran, too.

The family stopped, and the Kittens caught up to them. The little girl smiled shyly.

"Howdy, pardner," said the boy.

Donna laughed. "Howdy!"

Nanea knelt down in front of the little girl. "This

is for you." Nanea placed her lei over the little girl's head.

Donna did the same with the little boy, and Lily held out her lei to the mother.

"Oh, that's so sweet." The mother fumbled with her pocketbook.

"No, no," Nanea said, standing up. "These are gifts."

The mother smiled warmly. She bent down so Lily could place the lei over her head. "Thank you," she said. "*Mahalo.*"

As the Kittens watched them climb the gangplank, the band began to play "Aloha 'Oe." One sweet voice rose above all the other sounds, casting the lyrics over the crowd like a fisherman's net. This was one of the songs Queen Liliuokalani had written! Nanea's arms were suddenly covered with little bumps. She got chicken skin hearing this music!

The mother paused at the ship's rail to wave, and the children waved, too. The Kittens waved back.

"That was a good idea, Nanea," Donna said.

"I hated seeing those sad faces," Nanea answered.

"I just realized something," Lily said. "The first task

for the contest was to do a good deed for a stranger."

"*Kokua*," Donna said, using the Hawaiian word for a good deed.

Giving the leis to the family *was* kokua. Nanea hadn't even been thinking about the contest. But why couldn't it be both?

"Only three tasks to go," Nanea said. "And plenty of time, too."

❋

When she got home, Nanea plunked down on the porch and told Mele everything about Boat Day— especially the happy smile on the little girl's face.

Auntie Rose arrived home, fanning her face with her hat. "I'd love to sit and talk story," she called, "but Mrs. Santos is coming for supper, and I have so much to do!" She went inside her cottage, where Nanea could hear the rattle of pots and pans.

"Auntie Rose helped me with my contest." Nanea leaned her head against Mele's. "So I should do kokua for her, too, as a thank-you, right?"

Mele didn't answer but wandered over and sniffed at the hose curled up like a sleeping snake next to Auntie Rose's house.

"Great idea, Mele!" Every evening after selling leis, Auntie Rose sprayed the red dirt in her yard to settle the dust. Since she was cooking supper for company, Nanea could help out by doing the spraying. That would make Auntie Rose so happy! Nanea ran over to turn on the faucet. Mele's tail thumped in the red dirt.

Nanea pressed her thumb against the hose opening to make a spray. She swung her arm back and forth, back and forth across the yard. When she finished, it looked exactly like it did after Auntie Rose sprayed.

Nanea giggled. She would knock on Auntie Rose's door and then run away. Auntie Rose would never know who had done kokua for her. She might think it was the *menehune*, island leprechauns!

Nanea tiptoed across the yard, the damp red dirt cool under her bare feet. She crept up the steps, with Mele at her heels. Delicious dinner smells wafted out of the cottage. She stretched out her arm. *Knock, knock, knock.* Nanea leaped off the porch and dashed home. But Mele didn't dash with her. She stayed on Auntie Rose's front porch, sniffing. When Auntie Rose opened the door, Mele bolted inside!

"Oh, you naughty dog!" Auntie Rose cried. "You're

tracking mud all over my clean floors!"

Nanea peered around a palm tree and gasped. She saw her own footprints on the porch, and a line of paw prints inside Auntie Rose's house. Nanea turned around and skedaddled straight home.

"Hey there." Papa caught her as she bolted toward her bedroom. His hair was all mussed up from sleeping. He was just getting up for his night shift at the shipyard. "What's the hurry?"

Nanea meant to say, "nothing," but one look at Papa's blue eyes and everything came tumbling out.

Papa was quiet. "So you think running away will solve this pickle?" he finally asked.

She hung her head. "I don't know," she whispered.

He brushed her hair away from her face. "Oh, Nanea. Always in such a hurry to help. You need to think before you act," he said gently.

Nanea took a deep breath. Papa often told her that.

"How can you make things right?" Papa asked.

Nanea imagined the muddy paw prints all over Auntie Rose's floor. "Mop up the mess?"

"Sounds like a good plan."

"Won't Auntie Rose be mad at me?" Nanea asked.

"She might be a little," Papa admitted. "But she would be more upset if you didn't take responsibility for your actions. I would, too. Mistakes happen, but you can learn from them."

Papa sounded just like Tutu.

"A clean floor should help patch things up," he said. He wrapped his arms around Nanea and squeezed two times.

Nanea squeezed back. Then she went to get the mop from the closet.

Turkey Day

🌀 CHAPTER 3 🌀

On Thanksgiving morning, Nanea went to Lily's house. On the porch she removed her shoes and added them to the pile at the Sudas' front door. It was a Japanese custom that eventually became an island custom. No one wore shoes inside!

Donna was there, and the girls practiced the hula they planned to perform for their families. Nanea had made it up, with help from Mary Lou, and had taught it to her friends. Rather, *tried* to teach them. Nanea was starting to understand why it was such an honor to be a kumu hula. Nanea demonstrated again. "Forward two steps; then back two. Like this."

"I'll never get it right." Donna flopped onto Lily's bed. "I'm a better audience than a dancer."

"Come on!" Lily said. "We're helping Nanea

show appreciation for her family. For the contest. Remember?"

Donna groaned.

"How about this?" Nanea pointed to herself. "I'll do the whole dance and tell you the story as I go. When you understand the story, it's easier to do the dance."

"I'll try anything," Donna said.

Nanea put the needle back down on the record. Music filled the room, and she began to explain. "It's all about our families doing their daily routines." She pressed the edges of her hands together in a V, creating a sign for "book" to represent school. For Papa and Mr. Hill, she pantomimed pulling a welding visor over her face. For Uncle Fudge, she reeled in a fish, and for the mothers she danced through cooking motions. She even included Mele wagging her tail.

"At the end, everyone gathers around a big table," Nanea said, spreading her arms wide. Then she scooped her arms to her chest. "We are all together."

"That was so pretty!" Lily said.

Nanea tugged Donna to her feet.

"Are you sure I can't just be a palm tree?" Donna begged.

After they went through the dance once more, Nanea noticed the clock on Lily's nightstand. "Oh, I've got to go. I promised to help Mom. See you Kittens later!"

As she hurried down the street, Nanea heard planes from Hickam Field fly maneuvers overhead. Nanea shielded her eyes to watch the B-17Ds. Papa said they were called Flying Fortresses because they were so huge. She waved in case any of the pilots could see her.

The soft breeze carried so many good smells: the sweetness of garden flowers and fruit trees, but also the smoky smell of neighborhood *imu* fires. Her mouth watered to think of the *kalua* pig cooking in the pit Papa had dug in their backyard.

"I'm home!" Nanea called. She found her sister, mother, and grandmother in the kitchen. Tutu was pounding the *taro* with an old stone poi pounder. She motioned Nanea closer so they could greet in the traditional way, pressing foreheads and noses together and taking a deep breath. This was the *ha* part of aloha, the breath. The other part, *alo*, meant to share, to be close. Tutu had taught her that this meant they were breathing each other's essence.

Nanea turned her cheek to catch the regular kiss that would follow. Then, stepping around Mele's empty food dish, she snuck a tiny taste of the purple poi. It was sweet on her tongue. "So 'ono!" She reached out for another taste, and Tutu playfully batted her hand away.

"You'll ruin your supper," she said. But she was smiling.

"Just one more bite?" Nanea begged.

Tutu laughed. "I can never say no to you, Nanea."

"Nobody can." Mary Lou stirred the mayonnaise into the macaroni salad. "That's how it is when you're the baby."

Nanea's good mood popped like a balloon. She gave Mary Lou the stink eye.

"Why don't you arrange the flowers for the table?" Mom handed her a hollowed-out pineapple. "David carved this for a vase."

Nanea took the pineapple and stomped outside. *Wait until I win that contest*, she thought, yanking hibiscus blossoms off the nearest bush. *Then Mary Lou will stop calling me a baby once and for all.* Nanea looked down. Crumpled blossoms lay at her feet. Papa's words came back to her: "Think before you act!" Nanea took a deep breath and tried to calm down.

She gathered the unbruised blossoms, then snipped some ginger and a coconut palm branch. She separated the leafy parts of the branch from the ribs with her thumbnail and added the delicately draping ribs to the rest of the flowers.

"Very pretty," Tutu Kane said from a wicker rocker on the lanai. He winked. "The flowers are nice, too!"

Nanea giggled. Tutu Kane kidded around like Papa did. Her grandfather rubbed his knees. "These old bones needed a rest."

"Your bones aren't old!"

"Oh, yes they are. But in here," Tutu Kane tapped his chest, "I'm still young like you."

Nanea put the pineapple vase on a table and then sat on the porch next to her grandfather. "Tell me about hiking on the lava flows when you were my age," Nanea asked. She loved Tutu Kane's stories.

"After digging around all day, my friends and I would come home with our pockets full of Hawaiian diamonds—"

"Really, mica," Nanea interrupted.

"Mica, yes. But sparkled like diamonds."

"What else did you do?" Nanea asked.

"My parents would drive the two-lane dirt road up to 'Ewa, stopping along the way so we kids could fill sacks with little bitty tomatoes and berries, all growing wild by the road."

Nanea's mouth puckered up at the mention of the berries; the ones Tutu Kane had picked were plenty sour!

"And so many birds." Tutu Kane cupped his hand behind his ear. "We didn't need radio. Not with nature's symphony around us. Too much noise now. Cars. Planes. People." He sighed and got up from the chair. "I'll take the flowers inside."

Nanea tilted her head back and listened for the birdsong symphony, grateful that Tutu Kane lived close enough to teach her such things. She couldn't imagine living so far away from family, like Papa did.

Papa came out of the house. He picked up an armload of long, green ti leaves and walked to the imu fire in the yard.

"Do you miss Oregon, Papa?" Nanea asked, following him.

"You kids keep me too happy to be homesick." He fed the leaves to the fire. Then he looked at Nanea. "But I so wish your grandparents could see what a lovely girl you're growing up to be." He brushed off his hands. "Time to set up the croquet game. Fudge thinks he's going to beat me this time!"

Papa whistled cheerfully as he tapped the wickets in with a croquet mallet. Nanea imagined he must feel a tiny bit sad about being so far from home. As she watched him work, she got a terrific idea for bringing his Oregon family closer.

She hurried to her room and pulled her project box out from under her bed. Mele pawed at Nanea's leg as she removed the supplies she needed.

"Not now, girl," Nanea said, stapling several sheets of paper together to make a book. Then she reached for her crayons.

Every Thanksgiving, Papa shared the same story about the time his father brought home a young turkey. Papa named the turkey Fido because he came running like a dog when anyone whistled. Thanks to Papa's care, Fido was good and plump by the time November rolled around.

Nanea giggled as she drew Fido's round tummy. Mele tried to climb into Nanea's lap, but Nanea shooed her away. Nanea colored Fido's skinny legs orange. After dotting lots of freckles on Papa's face, she topped his head off with bright red hair.

When Papa told his story, he explained that even though he was a farm boy, he could not bear to think of Fido as dinner. Two days before Thanksgiving, he took Fido and hid in the woods. Grandpop found him late that night; Grandmom had been worried sick.

On the last page of the book, Nanea drew Papa's whole family—Grandpop, Grandmom, Uncle Frank, and Papa—sitting around a table loaded with good things to eat. But no turkey. Giggling again, she added a fifth chair to the table. She drew Fido sitting there with everyone else. He ended up being Papa's pet, living to the grand old age of ten.

"The end," Nanea wrote. "What do you think, Mele?"

Mele whined.

"Well, I think Papa will like it." Nanea went outside to look for him.

"What's this?" Papa asked when Nanea handed

him the book. After he finished reading it, Papa
swung her around. "My story is even better with your
pictures."

"I thought it would help you feel closer to home,"
Nanea said.

"You are my home, sweetheart." Papa kissed the
top of her head. "And boy am I thankful for you."

An hour later, Donna and her parents arrived.
Auntie Rose came over, and then Lily's family filled
the house. "Ready to lose at croquet?" Uncle Fudge
called out. Lily carried Aunt Betty's sweet potato
casserole into the kitchen and set it next to Mrs. Hill's
wiggly Jell-O salad and Auntie Rose's homemade
crescent rolls.

"Not too much longer till dinner!" Mom called as
she carved the turkey and arranged slices on a large
platter.

"Do we have time to do our hula?" Nanea asked.

"Just enough," said Tutu.

The Kittens quickly changed. Nanea had let Donna
and Lily pick something from her performance outfits.

Donna had chosen a blue-and-white fabric top, and Lily had picked a red-and-white one. Nanea wore a yellow-and-white top, and they each wore one of the ti-leaf skirts Nanea had made.

David and Tutu Kane strummed their ukuleles while everyone gathered in the backyard. When Nanea gave the signal, David and Tutu played the first notes of "*Lei E*: Wear This Lei."

Nanea did two hip rotations. Donna and Lily tried to keep up, but they forgot to join in. "Dance!" she urged.

"What's next?" Lily whispered.

"Scooping hands," Nanea whispered back, and six Kitten hands reached wide and then scooped to their hearts. Nanea was about to move into the final hand pose when . . . *CRASH!*

The music stopped. Mom raced inside, and everyone followed. "Oh, no!" Mom cried.

The turkey was all over the kitchen floor, and Mele was wolfing down the meat. Nanea gasped.

"She managed to knock the platter off the counter," said Auntie Rose.

Mom shooed Mele away. "It's ruined."

"Mele usually has such nice manners," Tutu said.

Mom picked up the platter and then looked at Nanea. "You fed her this morning, right?"

Nanea had been so busy with practicing her hula and making the flower arrangement and her project for Papa that she'd completely forgotten that important job. That's what Mele had been trying to tell her while she was working on Papa's book. She was hungry! Nanea hung her head.

"I guess we're carrying on the Mitchell tradition of a no-turkey Thanksgiving dinner," Papa said. He showed the book Nanea had made to Uncle Fudge. "I've told you this story, right?"

Uncle Fudge said, "Only fifty times!"

"More like a hundred," chuckled Auntie Rose.

"Thank goodness there's kalua pig," said David.

"And salads," Mary Lou said.

"And desserts," added Donna.

"Come on, Kittens," called Mrs. Hill. "Let's set the table."

Mom was smiling, but her words to Nanea were firm. "I guess this means you'll be in charge of kitchen cleanup."

Nanea tugged at her skirt. "I'm sorry," she said. She *had* let Mele go hungry, and that had caused the big mess.

"Go change," Mom said kindly. "We still have a feast to eat."

As Nanea turned to go to her room, Tutu placed a hibiscus behind Nanea's ear. "You're a beautiful dancer," she said. "And a beautiful child."

Nanea sighed. She didn't want to be a child. She wanted to be grown-up. That would never happen if she didn't stop messing up.

The other two Kittens refused to let Nanea clean up by herself. After dinner, the girls took turns washing, rinsing, and drying the dishes. David and Mary Lou were outside playing croquet with Lily's brothers, and the adults were in the living room having coffee when Donna said, "Hey, I have a great joke. Knock, knock."

"Who's there?" Lily asked.

But before Donna could answer, Nanea shushed her. The grown-ups' voices had gotten quiet. Nanea went to lean against the kitchen doorway to listen.

"The negotiations with the Japanese aren't going well," Mr. Hill said.

"They have to!" Mom insisted. "If they don't . . ." but her voice just trailed off.

"It would be madness if the Japanese didn't cooperate," Tutu Kane said.

"I'm worried," said Uncle Fudge.

"Everything will be fine," said Aunt Betty. "The Japanese don't want to go to war with America."

"If negotiations are going badly, I'm not sure if we'll be able to stay out of the fight," Mr. Hill replied.

"The diplomats will work things out," Mom said confidently. "Betty's right. The last thing Japan wants is a war with the United States."

"I agree," Tutu added.

"I hope you're right," Papa said. "Now, who wants to help me cover up the barbecue pit?"

The other men volunteered to go with Papa. There was a clattering of cups as Mom poured more coffee for the women.

Nanea went back to the sink. She scrubbed the last dirty pot extra hard. "Did you hear all that?" she asked Lily and Donna.

"What? About the war?" Donna blew a bubble and snapped it. "I don't listen to any of that."

But Lily was curious. "What about it?" she asked.

Nanea gave the pot one last scrub. She thought about telling them that Uncle Fudge was worried. But grown-ups worried all the time about stuff that didn't happen. Mom and Papa worried about David getting a ticket when he drove his old jalopy, but he never did. Tutu Kane fretted that he and Tutu were getting too old to run Pono's Market, but they still worked in the shop every day.

Nanea let the water out of the sink. "Nothing," she replied. She repeated what Aunt Betty had said. "Everything will be fine."

A SKY FULL
OF PLANES

o matter how long I've lived here, I still can't get used to being at the beach in December," Donna said. "It feels too warm for Christmas."

Nanea had written "Kittens" in the sand. Now she added the date. December 6, 1941. "The Matson Christmas tree ship should be here this week," she said. "Then it will really seem like the holidays."

"I can't wait!" Lily did a happy spin in the sand. "I love the smell of fir trees."

Donna picked up the Brownie camera her grandmother had sent for an early Christmas present and aimed it at what Nanea had written. "That's going to make a keen snapshot for my Kittens album."

So far, every picture Donna had taken that day—even David's slippers at the water's edge—was "keen."

"You know what would really be keen?" Nanea said. "Shave ice!"

"Good idea!" Lily rubbed her tummy.

Nanea scuffed across the beach to where Mary Lou and her friend Iris shared a towel, watching the surfers. David was on the water somewhere; Nanea squinted to pick out his longboard. There he was, riding the waves with ease, like the famous surfer, Duke Kahanamoku!

"May I please have my coin purse?" Nanea held out her hand.

It was Iris who reached for Mary Lou's beach bag. "Off for shave ice?"

Nanea nodded.

"Sounds 'ono," Mary Lou said. "But I don't feel like moving."

"Ha!" Nanea kicked sand on her sister's legs. "It's more like you don't feel like taking your eyes off Al!" Mary Lou hadn't done a very good job of hiding her crush on Iris's big brother.

"Oh you!" Mary Lou jumped up to chase Nanea.

Nanea pranced out of her way.

Iris giggled.

"Looks like it's time for someone to take a dunk!"

Mary Lou said, lunging at Nanea. Nanea zigzagged across the sand, steps ahead of her sister. She ran up to Lily and grabbed her arm. "Home base," she called, gasping for breath. "I'm safe."

"You goof." Mary Lou tugged her hair. "Come straight back after getting the shave ice, okay?"

"Aye-aye!" Nanea saluted, and the Kittens skipped to the shave ice stand.

"I'll have lemon, please," Lily said. Lily always ordered lemon. The shave ice man mounded the tiny ice crystals into a paper cup, picked up the bottle of yellow syrup, and drizzled it over the ice.

"Orange, please," Donna said, choosing her favorite flavor.

Nanea ordered strawberry, as usual. She handed the man enough coins for all three shave ices and then took her pink-tinted cone. Soon her tongue would be barber-pole red. That was the best part of choosing strawberry.

The girls shuffled back to their towels, wiggling their toes through the warm top layer of sand to find some cool beneath.

"How are you doing on the Helping Hands

contest?" Donna asked between bites.

"Isn't the deadline coming up?" Lily asked as she settled, cross-legged, on her towel.

"December fifteenth. Nine days." Nanea licked syrup from her fingers. "But I've been so busy with homework and practicing hula for the Christmas performance at the USO that it's been hard to find time to work on the contest."

"You have two tasks to do, right?" Donna asked.

Nanea sat down, too. "The two hardest: Make a difference in my community, and turn trouble into triumph."

"Trouble into triumph," Donna repeated. "Thanksgiving was trouble, right?"

"It sure was," agreed Nanea. She let the shave ice trickle down her throat, thinking about the ruined turkey.

"What if you turned *that* into triumph?" Lily asked. "What about making a nice meal for your family to make up for the ruined one?"

"Way to use the old noggin," Donna encouraged.

Lily stretched out her legs, digging her toes into the sand. "My mom likes breakfast in bed."

"But how could I make breakfast in bed for everyone?" Nanea sighed. She had visions of spilling pancake syrup on her parents or splashing milk and Corn Flakes on Mary Lou and David.

"What if you just make breakfast?" Donna asked.

Lily nodded. "You could make something special—"

"And decorate the table—" Donna added.

"What a keen idea, Kittens!" Then Nanea's smile faded. "But I'm not allowed to use the stove by myself."

"Maybe you could trade something with Auntie Rose for a plate of her malasadas," Donna suggested.

"And you could serve papaya and cold cereal, like they do at the Royal Hawaiian," Lily added.

"You two are the best!" Nanea said. "I'll get up early tomorrow and set everything out. I'll squeeze fresh lemon juice on the papayas, too, the way Papa likes. And I'll do all the cleaning up after."

"You have lots of practice with cleaning up," Lily teased.

"You can say that again," Nanea agreed.

❁

Auntie Rose was happy to trade the basket of
plumeria Nanea had picked for a batch of malasadas.
Nanea borrowed Auntie's alarm clock, too, so she
wouldn't oversleep. When it rang the next morning,
she turned it off quickly so it wouldn't wake Mary Lou.
But Nanea shouldn't have worried. Her sister could
sleep through anything.

Nanea set the table, placing the platter of sweet,
puffy malasadas right in the center. And to make it
really fancy, she'd made a place card for each person.

Something was missing. Oh! Mom always deco-
rated with flowers for special occasions. Nanea felt
very responsible to have thought of that. This breakfast
would certainly show her family that their "baby" was
growing up!

She popped into the backyard to cut some pink
and red hibiscus. The early morning air was fresh
and clean. Nanea could smell the delicate yellow blossoms of the ginger plants from Mrs. Lin's garden. They
would be pretty on the table, too, and Mrs. Lin never
minded sharing. A little zebra dove perched on the
fence, cooing at Nanea as she snipped a handful of
ginger blooms. Nanea cooed back, and they had a

cheerful conversation about that shiny new bike Nanea was going to win in the contest.

Startled by a loud rumbling sound, the little bird flew off. Nanea was startled, too: What *was* making that racket? She looked up. The sky was dotted with planes, flying in formation. Nothing new. Yet something was different. Why were they flying so low? One plane dipped down, down, down, and Nanea could see a round red sun on its tail. Every school kid on the island knew what that red "meatball" meant: Japanese Zeros! Those were fighter planes!

One loud boom after another after another shattered the quiet morning. In the distance, toward Wheeler Airfield, thick columns of oily black punched bruises in the blue sky. Nanea screamed.

David flew out of the house and snatched Nanea back inside.

"Wh-wh-what's happening?" Nanea asked. Her teeth were chattering.

David carried her to the sofa. "I don't know," he said. Mom held her close as Nanea described what she'd seen.

Papa switched on the radio.

"It's eight-oh-four a.m., and this is your KGMB announcer, interrupting this program to recall all Army, Navy, and Marine Corps personnel to duty."

Mom tucked one of Tutu's crocheted afghans around her, but Nanea still shivered.

Everyone stayed glued to the radio for the next fifteen minutes while the announcer called twice more for military personnel to report to duty. Then police officers and firefighters were ordered to report. But there was no explanation for what Nanea had seen.

"I better get to the shipyard." Papa jumped up and ran to the phone. Nanea heard him call Mr. Hill. "Have you heard?" Papa barked. "Be ready in five minutes."

"But you're not military," Mom protested when Papa hung up.

"I'm sure they'll need civilian workers, too," Papa said, pulling on his coveralls and work boots. Minutes later, he roared away in their sedan.

Nanea glanced at the clock. It was eight thirty-five. Her family was supposed to be at the kitchen table now, enjoying the special breakfast she'd prepared. It seemed hours ago that she'd cut flowers for the table. Despite the warm afghan, Nanea trembled as if she were sitting in the icebox.

Papa had barely been gone five minutes when another announcer shouted into the microphone. *"This is no maneuver. This is the real McCoy. Enemy airplanes have attacked."*

THE REAL MCCOY

❧ CHAPTER 5 ❧

anea squeezed against the sofa cushions, making herself as small as possible.

Enemy airplanes! Those *were* Japanese Zeros she'd seen.

David ran down the hall just as Mary Lou padded into the living room, rubbing her eyes. "What's going on?" she asked sleepily.

"It's an attack," Nanea said. With those words, she started to cry.

"Attack?" Mary Lou looked at Mom. "What is she talking about?"

Mom rubbed her forehead. "It . . . it sounds as if Nanea's right."

Mary Lou stared. "I don't understand. How? Who?"

"So far, all we know is that enemy planes have

attacked the island." Mom swallowed hard. "Planes with rising suns on them."

"The Japanese?" Mary Lou wrapped her arms around herself. "But we talked about it in class last week. There were negotiations in Washington. Things were supposed to work out."

Fire truck sirens growled in the distance. Nanea edged closer to Mom.

"The man on the radio said all military personnel had to report to their stations," Nanea said. She didn't bother to wipe away her tears. "But Papa left, too. And Mr. Hill."

Mary Lou covered her face with her hands. "Turn the radio up," she said. "Maybe there's an update."

Mom edged off the couch to adjust the volume, and the three of them listened intently. David rushed back into the living room, buttoning his Boy Scout shirt.

"I'm going to report to my post at the VFW hall. That's what we're supposed to do in an emergency," he said, brushing Mom's cheek with a kiss. "Don't know when I'll be back."

"You'd better ride your bike," Mom said. "They just told civilians to keep their cars off the roads." Then she grabbed David's arm and held it. "Be safe, son."

"I will." David looked at Nanea. "Don't worry about me," he said, flashing his Hollywood smile.

After David left, Nanea jumped off the sofa and ran to the front window. Pressing her nose against the glass, she watched her brother pedal away until he was no bigger than a papaya seed.

"Mom, Mom!" Mary Lou shouted, cranking the volume knob on the radio. Mom's favorite KGMB announcer, Webley Edwards, was speaking.

"Listen carefully. The island of Oahu is being attacked by enemy planes. The center of this attack is Pearl Harbor, but the planes are attacking airfields as well. Now keep your radio on and tell your neighbors to do the same. I repeat. We are under attack by enemy planes."

"David!" Nanea pounded her hand on the window. "Come back!" But he was gone.

"The attack's at Pearl Harbor." Mary Lou fell to her knees in front of the radio.

"Pearl Harbor?" Nanea trembled all over with a sudden realization. "That's where Papa went."

Mom pulled Nanea away from the window. "He'll be fine," she said firmly. "David, too."

With all her heart, Nanea wanted to believe those words.

Mom reached for the telephone and began to dial.

"Mother! Are you all right?" Mom put her hand to her cheek as she listened. "Oh, that's awful."

Nanea wondered what was awful.

"But you and Dad are okay?" Mom grasped the receiver so tight, her knuckles turned white. "Thank goodness. Thank goodness."

Nanea held her mother's free hand, leaning in to breathe her comforting smell of lemon and coffee.

"You need to come here," Mom said. "Right away. Richard's gone to the shipyard." She listened, nodded, listened some more. "Better plan to stay. Who knows what we're up against."

Mom hung up the phone. Nanea had been concentrating so hard on her mother's conversation that she hadn't been aware of the sirens, which were roaring louder and louder. She shivered, remembering the thick black plumes of smoke smudging the blue, blue sky.

"The radio announcer just told us to fill our bathtubs with water," Mary Lou said. "Buckets, too. In case the Japanese cut off our water supply." She jumped up from the floor and dashed to the bathroom.

Nanea froze in front of the radio, afraid to miss another word. The announcer was speaking in his smooth-as-butter voice, as if talking about the price of pineapples or sugar. *"Here is a warning to all people through the Territory of Hawaii and especially the island of Oahu. In the event of an air raid, stay under cover. I repeat. If an air raid should begin, do not go out of doors. Stay under cover."*

A rapping at the front door made Nanea jump a mile. It was Auntie Rose. "Everyone okay?" she asked.

Mom grabbed her hand. "Yes. You?"

"There are a few bullet holes in my kitchen walls," Auntie Rose said in disbelief. "But I'm alright."

Mom's face paled. Nanea stared. Bullet holes? Right next door? She shivered even harder.

Auntie Rose stepped closer. "Don't you fret. The planes are gone now." Her voice was light, but Nanea could tell that she was worried. Auntie Rose tugged the afghan tighter around Nanea before glancing over at Mom. "How are your folks?" she asked.

Mom leaned in to whisper to Auntie Rose. Nanea heard her say, "It came through the neighbor's roof."

Nanea wondered what "it" was. More bullets?

Auntie Rose shook her head. "Why did they do this?"

"Because of the military bases here?" Mom guessed. "All the ships and planes . . ." Her voice dwindled.

"Don't they know what it will mean?" Auntie Rose sat heavily on the sofa.

Nanea remembered overhearing the grown-ups' conversation at Thanksgiving. She jerked her head toward Mom.

Mom only pressed her lips together and stared at the radio.

"Can I go see Lily?" Nanea asked, heading toward the front door. Lily hated sirens. She'd be so frightened.

"NO!" Mom shouted. "I mean," she said, softening her voice, "no one goes outside."

But Auntie Rose went outside to come over here, Nanea thought. *And David and Papa went outside to help. And Tutu and Tutu Kane are outside right now, driving to our house.* She didn't give voice to her thoughts. It didn't seem right to argue with Mom. Not now.

Mom kissed the top of Nanea's head. "I'm going to make some coffee," she said. When Mom walked into the kitchen, she saw the table and Nanea's breakfast surprise. "Did you do this, Nanea? It looks lovely, honey. Can you eat a little something?"

But Nanea just shook her head. She couldn't eat when she was so upset.

"The bathtub's filled," Mary Lou reported.

Mom pulled several buckets out of the broom closet. "Fill these, too, please." She brushed her hair back from her face. "I need to gather up blankets to cover the windows. The radio just announced that there will be a blackout tonight." She bustled off without even explaining what a blackout was.

Nanea didn't know what to do. She went back to the living room and sat in front of the radio, hoping to hear some good news. But there wasn't any. Mary Lou came and sat with her while Mom and Auntie Rose spoke quietly in the kitchen.

Nearly two hours passed before Tutu Kane and Tutu finally arrived. Nanea and Mary Lou ran to the door to help their grandparents with their bags.

"Mahalo, keiki." Tutu moved slowly, like a landbound sea turtle. "My heart is so heavy. All this damage to our beautiful island."

"What took you so long?" Nanea asked. Her grandparents lived close enough that Nanea could walk
there in fifteen minutes.

"We drove at a snail's pace," Tutu Kane explained.
"The roads are packed with cars. People, too."

In a low voice, Tutu added, "We passed a sedan
that was covered with bullet holes."

Nanea shivered.

"The Reyes' house on Hauoli Street lost its roof,"
Tutu Kane said, referring to a good customer at Pono's
Market.

"What about your store?" Auntie Rose asked.

"We called Mr. Lopez," Tutu Kane replied. "His
bakery is next to Pono's, and he was able to check on
our shops. Both are fine. No damage."

"What a relief!" Mom murmured.

"And he said he would keep an eye on things until
we could get there." Tutu Kane paused. "Who knows
when that will be?"

"The market is safe, but others weren't so lucky."
Tutu let out such a heavy sigh that Nanea could
practically feel it from where she stood. "Several
stores in the McCully neighborhood burned to the

ground. There was even a fire at the school."

"Which school?" Mary Lou asked.

Tutu Kane shook his head sadly. "Lunalilo," he whispered.

Mom put her arm around Nanea. For a moment, Nanea couldn't breathe. "My school is on fire?"

Tutu smoothed her hair. "Don't worry."

Everyone was telling her that. But how could she not worry? Nanea's legs gave way. Tutu caught her and pulled her into her ample lap.

"Shh, shh," Tutu soothed.

Nanea couldn't bear to think about her classroom with its spinning globe and bright red pencil sharpener and colorful world map. All gone. She started to cry again.

"You're safe here," Tutu murmured.

Home had always been the safest place in the world. But within a few short hours, everything in Nanea's life had been turned upside down. She squeezed her eyes shut, trying only to see the beautiful things: palm trees, sandy beaches, fat white clouds. But all the images were edged in black.

Nanea's eyes popped open. Instead of news, a

crackling static filled the room "What happened to the radio?"

"KGMB's off the air," Mary Lou said. "KGU, too." She turned the radio dial back and forth, but there was nothing.

Not one sound at all.

MISSING

here was nothing to do but wait. They all sat, ears straining to hear some news. Any news! But the radio stations were silent. Every one of them was off the air. Outside, Nanea could hear cars honking and sirens wailing, but somehow the quiet inside was even more frightening.

"Honey," Mom said to Nanea, "could you carry your grandparents' bags to your room?"

Nanea did as she was asked, knowing she'd miss more grown-up talk. Sure enough, as soon as she was out of sight, the murmuring started. *Why did Mary Lou get to stay and listen?* Nanea wondered.

Nanea was happy to give up her bedroom for Tutu and Tutu Kane. Having her grandparents in the house made her feel safer, and it meant there were two fewer people to worry about. She blinked away thoughts of Papa and David. They were strong and smart and brave. David's Hawaiian middle name was Kekoa, which meant "warrior." *Nothing will happen to him,* she told herself. *Or Papa.* A tear slid down her cheek anyway.

Nanea set the bags down. It was a good thing she didn't have to shoo Mele off her pillow. Tutu believed dogs belonged outside. But where was Mele? She always napped on Nanea's pillow.

"Mele?" Nanea called. "Did the noises and the sirens scare you?" Nanea peeked under her bed and in her closet. She checked under Mom and Papa's bed and even looked in David's room.

Nanea went to the kitchen, calling, "Here, girl!" She tried to remember when she had last seen Mele. Had she gone out in the yard while Nanea picked flowers? Nanea searched the whole house, but there was no Mele. Nanea was starting to panic. She ran to the front door and opened it.

"Nanea!" Mom called. "Stop! Stay inside."

But it wasn't Mom's voice that made Nanea stop. It was Lily's. She was in her front yard, screaming.

"No! Daddy! No!"

Nanea had never heard her friend sound so frightened.

Two men in dark suits and fedora hats were leading Uncle Fudge to a black sedan parked at the curb. They looked like mobsters from the gangster movie the Kittens had seen a few weeks back. Lily ran after them, pleading. "Don't take him!"

Nanea started to go to Lily, but Mom held her back.

Ignoring Lily, the two men put Uncle Fudge in the backseat of the car and drove away.

"Stay here," Mom instructed before she hurried across the street and down the block to the Sudas' house. Nanea ran after her. Tutu and Auntie Rose ran after Nanea.

Lily was standing at the curb, crying. Nanea went to her, and Lily grabbed Nanea's hand.

"They took Daddy away," Lily sobbed.

Nanea did not understand what was happening. She turned to the front porch, where Aunt Betty stood twisting a dish towel around and around.

"They didn't even take off their shoes before barging in," she said.

Mom gently steered Aunt Betty into the house, and

Nanea led Lily back into the living room.

Aunt Betty wiped her tears with the towel. "I don't know what to do, May," she said to Nanea's mom.

Nanea wasn't sure what to do either. Lily sat down in her father's chair and began picking at a frayed thread on the arm. Tears rolled quietly down her face. Nanea got her friend a handkerchief and then squeezed next to her on the chair. Lily blew her nose. Nanea couldn't find any words to say.

"I could've stopped them," Tommy said, waving his toy six-shooters. "But Mother wouldn't let me."

"Put those toy guns away, Tommy," said Aunt Betty.

Tutu got out some building blocks, stacking them into a tall tower. "Want to knock this down?" she asked.

Tommy did. Then Tutu built another tower. Soon Tommy was laughing as he knocked down the blocks as quickly as Tutu stacked them.

Lily's big brother Gene stared out the window. "They were FBI."

"What would the FBI want with your father?" Mom asked.

Aunt Betty shook her head.

Mom looked from Aunt Betty to Gene. "This must be a big mistake," said Mom.

"It's no mistake," Gene burst out. "It's because he looks like the enemy."

What did Gene be mean? Nanea wondered. How could anyone ever think someone as good and kind as Uncle Fudge could look like an enemy?

"Calm down, please," Aunt Betty said. "This *is* a mistake, and we'll get it straightened out."

Auntie Rose came out of the kitchen with a cup of tea for Aunt Betty. She had made sandwiches for the rest of the family, but no one wanted to eat.

"I know a lawyer who may be able to help," Nanea's mom said. She jumped up. "I'll try to call him right now." Aunt Betty and Auntie Rose followed her into the kitchen.

"I'm scared," Lily whispered. "What if your mom is wrong? What if we can't get this straightened out? What's going to happen to my dad? To our family?" Fresh tears made tracks down her cheeks.

"I'm scared, too," Nanea confessed. She told Lily what she'd seen from the backyard that morning, whispering so that Tommy wouldn't hear. "Everything is so mixed up," she said. "Papa and David both went off to help, and now your dad is gone, and . . ." Nanea's voice trailed off.

"What?" Lily asked.

"I can't find Mele," Nanea answered. And with that, she started to cry.

Lily took her hand and squeezed it tight.

Mom came out of the kitchen. "Come on, Nanea. We'd best get home." She turned to hug Aunt Betty. "I'll check on you later."

Aunt Betty nodded. "Thank you."

Even though Auntie Rose lived right next to Nanea's house, Tutu insisted that they walk her home. "We look out for our 'ohana," she explained. "Especially now."

As they left Auntie Rose's porch, Nanea felt like a tiny canoe on a choppy sea. There was only one cure when she felt like this: Mele. No matter how bad things were, that poi dog could always make her feel better.

Nanea wanted to go look for Mele, but Mom said they had to get inside. She put her arm around Nanea as they hurried up the porch steps. "She'll turn up."

"Her empty belly will bring her back," Tutu agreed,

holding the door open for Nanea.

Nanea looked up and down the street one last time. "Come home, Mele," she called sadly before going inside the house.

❀

Late that afternoon, Mom stood on a step stool in front of the living room window. "Nanea, can you please hand that to me?" she asked, pointing to a dark green blanket tossed over the couch.

"So what is a blackout?" Nanea asked as she handed Mom the blanket.

"It means there can't be any lights at night. Not in the stores or on the streets or in houses." Mom tacked one corner of the blanket above the window frame, then the other, completely covering the glass. "That's why we have to hang up dark fabric or paper."

"I don't get it," Nanea said. "What good is having it all dark?"

Mary Lou brought Mom another armful of blankets and towels. "If enemy planes return, there won't be any lights to help them find the island," she said.

Are the planes going to come back? Nanea wondered. She glanced at Mom.

"It's only a precaution," Mom said quickly. "Let's not borrow trouble. There's nothing to worry about."

Mom kept saying there was nothing to worry about, but Nanea thought there was plenty to worry about.

At six o'clock, when Mom turned out all the lights for the blackout, it was so dark inside the house that Nanea couldn't take two steps without bumping into something.

"If the windows are all covered, why can't we turn on a lamp?" Nanea asked.

"We can't take any chances," Mom explained in the dark. "There will be air raid wardens walking the neighborhoods, checking for any sign of light."

Nanea felt her way to the sofa and curled up. This time, instead of an afghan, she was wrapped up in fears and worries. *Would the planes come back? Would there be more bombs? Was Papa okay? And David? And Uncle Fudge? And where, oh where, was Mele?*

WAR

 thump woke Nanea the next morning. She bolted upright. "What was that? Are the Japanese planes back?"

"It's the newspaper being delivered, that's all." Mary Lou sat up on the other end of the sofa. "Just the paper."

Nanea blinked, confused about why she was on the couch with Mary Lou. Then she remembered. Tutu and Tutu Kane had slept in their bedroom. Nanea leaned over the edge of the sofa.

"Good morning, silly poi dog," she said. Then she remembered something else from the day before. Mele was missing.

"Maybe she came home last night," Mary Lou said encouragingly. "Let's go look!"

Nanea followed Mary Lou to the kitchen. Tutu

stood at the stove making eggs. Mom was dishing up rice. Tutu Kane came through the back door carrying the empty trash bin and the newspaper.

"Was Mele outside?" Mary Lou asked.

Tutu Kane shook his head.

"Has *anyone* seen her this morning?" Nanea's throat was so tight that it hurt to talk.

Mom set a plate on the table. "Honey, come eat breakfast. You'll feel better."

Nanea shook her head. "I won't feel better until Mele comes home."

"And that'll be soon," Mary Lou assured her.

"How about Papa or David?" Nanea asked, sitting down at the table. "Have they called?"

"I doubt they can use a phone. The lines are likely all tied up with emergencies," Mom said, rubbing her forehead. "But I know they'll check in as soon as they can."

"Fresh pineapple juice!" Tutu poured Nanea a glass. "Your favorite."

Nanea took a tiny sip, but the juice didn't ease the tightness in her throat. She sat, chin in hands, worrying.

Across the table, Tutu Kane unfolded the news-paper. The headline on the front page of the *Star-Bulletin* screamed: "War Declared on Japan by U.S."

"We're at war?" Nanea asked, her heart pounding.

"They attacked us," Mary Lou said. "What else could we do?"

Words jumped out at Nanea from the article. *Ships sunk. Sailors lost. Civilians killed.* She closed her eyes, unable to read any more.

Tutu Kane shook his head. "The Japanese generals must have known this would be the last straw."

Nanea's stomach felt like it did when she ate too many green mangoes. She bent over, feeling sick.

Tutu Kane saw her. He folded the paper, setting it aside. "This is for grown-ups to be concerned about." He nudged Nanea's plate closer to her. "Eat this good breakfast."

Nanea could barely chew one spoonful of rice. Tutu Kane was trying to protect her. She knew that. But this war wasn't just for grown-ups to think about. Kids were upset, too.

Mom placed some hard-boiled eggs in a hamper.

"Are we going on a picnic?" That seemed an

odd thing to do on a Monday morning. "What about school?"

"Closed," Mary Lou said, "until further notice, according to the paper."

"Because of the fire?" Nanea felt confused.

"Because of the attacks," Mary Lou explained. "All the schools are closed."

Nanea's stomach hurt even worse. "So we're having a picnic since there's no school?"

"Not a picnic," Mom said. "This is for Fudge."

"Is he home?" Nanea sat forward, eager for good news.

"No." Mom bit her lip. "But the lawyer I spoke to yesterday found out that he's at the immigration station. I'm going with Betty and the children today to see him."

"I want to go, too," Nanea said.

Mom sliced some pineapple upside down cake, adding it to the hamper. She looked at Nanea's plate. "Eat some breakfast first, and we'll see."

Nanea managed only two more bites with her stomach so full of troubles. "When are we leaving?" she asked.

"In about an hour," Mom answered.

"Can I go outside and look for Mele?" Nanea asked.

"Yes," Tutu Kane said. "But stay nearby."

Nanea could tell by Mom's face that she wasn't happy with Tutu Kane's answer. As she hurried out of the kitchen, Nanea heard Tutu Kane tell Mom, "Only orchids thrive indoors."

Nanea dressed as quickly as she could and then ran outside. At the bottom of the porch steps, she stopped and searched the sky. Not a plane in sight—friend or enemy. She let out a breath of relief. The smell of stale smoke overpowered the sweet fragrance of Mrs. Lin's ginger plants and the backyard mango trees. Even the mynah birds were silent.

She shivered a little, glancing back at her house. *Should I stay inside? It's safe there. No! I have to find Mele.* Summoning all her courage, Nanea walked to the end of Fern Street, then turned on McCully, calling Mele's name as she went. She turned left on Lime, walking down to Wiliwili and back. One big block. A whole lot of calling. She was turning onto McCully, toward home, when Mrs. Lin waved to her.

"Nanea!" Mrs. Lin called, waggling her cane. "You

are just the person I was hoping to see."

"Hello, Mrs. Lin." Nanea usually enjoyed chatting with her elderly neighbor, but there was nothing usual about today.

"I was wondering what you'd heard about Fudge." Mrs. Lin rapped her cane on the ground. "Do you know they arrested my doctor? And Reverend Osumi?"

"I didn't know." It hadn't occurred to Nanea that Uncle Fudge wasn't the only one the FBI had taken.

"And last night Mr. Lopez made me turn out the lamp in my kitchen." She shook her head. "Just because he's the air raid warden doesn't mean he can be so bossy!"

"Mom said the wardens are supposed to make sure everything is dark," Nanea explained. "It's an important job."

"One little lamp." Mrs. Lin sighed.

"I should probably go." Nanea was running out of time to look for Mele.

But Mrs. Lin kept talking. "Someone said there were Japanese workers cutting arrows through the sugarcane fields to guide the attacking planes." She tapped her cane on the ground again.

Nanea didn't know what to say. She couldn't believe anyone on the island would help the enemy. Who would lend a hand to destroy their home?

Before Nanea could reply, Mom called to her from the front porch. "It's time to leave."

"Go, go," Mrs. Lin waved her off.

Nanea ran toward the Sudas' car. She slid into the backseat with Lily. "What's that?" she asked, pointing at an envelope.

Lily sighed. "A letter for my dad."

"Aren't you going to talk to him?" Nanea asked.

Lily turned the envelope over and over in her hand. "Mother doesn't know if us kids will be allowed to see him. This is just in case."

"They have to let you see him," Nanea said.

Lily held the letter to her heart. "Were you out looking for Mele?"

Nanea fiddled with the window crank. "Yes, but there's no sign of her."

"No sign of her *yet*," Lily said. "She'll turn up."

That was just like Lily to encourage Nanea at a time like this. "Silly old poi dog," Nanea mumbled. She hid her tears by looking out the window.

Nanea was stunned at how her town had changed in only a day. Neighborhoods were dotted with burned buildings. A car rested upside down on the street. Reading about the damage in the newspaper was one thing. Seeing it with her own eyes made Nanea feel like she'd fallen off the playground swings and gotten the wind knocked out of her.

Gene drove a careful path through the pick-up-sticks mess of traffic and debris. A man crossed in front of them, pushing a wheelbarrow full of clumps of metal. He stopped every now and then to pick something up.

After a few more turns, Nanea caught sight of the Aloha Tower. The last time she'd seen the tower was on Boat Day, when the Kittens had given their leis to that family. On that day, it had seemed impossible for anything bad to happen to their island.

Gene pulled up to the immigration station and turned off the engine. No one moved for a moment. Then Aunt Betty opened the passenger door, and everyone got out.

"What's this?" a guard asked when he saw the

picnic hamper Mom was carrying.

Nanea shrank back, but Mom answered calmly. "Some lunch for my brother, Fumio Suda." She and Nanea had to pretend they were related to Uncle Fudge in order to see him.

"No outside food allowed." The guard tapped the gun on his belt.

Mom's voice was steady. "I think my brother would be happy to share our mother's homemade pineapple cake." Slowly, she reached into the basket and offered the guard a piece.

He glanced at it and then glanced behind him. "All right." He took the cake. "But I have to check this out." He poked through the hamper and then he waved them on.

Another guard led them down a hall and opened a heavy door to a small room. A disheveled man sat hunched over on the floor, his back to them.

"Daddy!" Lily called. The man turned, leaped up and swung her around. Nanea had never seen Uncle Fudge with whiskers. He always shaved no matter how early he got up to go fishing.

Tommy handed Uncle Fudge a drawing. "I made

this for you," he said, clinging to his father's leg.

Mom gave Uncle Fudge the hamper of food. "Thank you," he said. "I'll share this with the others."

He told them that the lawyer Mom called had already come and gone. "Thank you for sending him, May. I'm hopeful he can help. He says it's a mistake I'm here."

"It's because we're Japanese," Gene said.

"The mistake is that my name is similar to another's on the FBI watch list," Uncle Fudge said. He shook his head sadly. "If I get out, does that mean that other man must take my place?"

"We'll worry about that when the time comes," said Aunt Betty. She handed Uncle Fudge a shaving kit and a sweater. "I brought these."

Uncle Fudge bowed. "Thank you."

"Come along." Mom tugged Nanea's sleeve. "We'll let them have some family time."

Mom and Nanea waited in a little room down the hall, but not for very long. Lily was crying as she walked toward them. Nanea ran to her and gave her friend a hug.

"I hardly got any time to talk to Daddy," Lily said.

"Let's be grateful for the time we did have,"
Aunt Betty said, holding firmly to Tommy's hand.

Gene made a noise of disgust. But he didn't say
anything.

The pineapple cake guard nodded to them as they
left. "Take care." He sounded as if he meant it.

Nanea tried not to look out the window on the
drive home. She didn't need anything else to make her
sad. But when Gene turned off Kapiolani Boulevard,
there was Lunalilo. "Our school!" she cried.

Gene slowed down, and everyone stared at the
burned school with the gaping hole in the roof.

Nanea's eyes filled with tears. "The library must be
ruined!"

"It looks like everything's all wet," Lily added.

"From the fire hoses," Mom explained.

Nanea remembered the time she'd accidentally
dropped a library book in the bathtub, turning it into
a sodden mess. She'd had to save up for several weeks
to replace that book. How would the school replace an
entire library?

It looked like it wasn't just the library. Their
classroom, which was tucked right behind it, must

be damaged, too. Miss Smith's magical classroom. Images of their teacher's sweet smile and desks in neat rows and gold stars on papers flooded Nanea's memory. How could it be gone?

Lily sniffled. "I want to go home."

Gene pressed on the gas, and they drove away.

Nanea wanted to go home, too. But home—her beautiful island—wasn't the same. The puzzle pieces were in such a jumble. Would they ever be able to put them back together again?

LOST AND FOUND

anea was glad her grandparents were staying with them, but she wasn't too happy about sharing the sofa with her sister. Mary Lou never seemed to stop moving, so she was always kicking Nanea. In the middle of the third night, Nanea crawled off the sofa and made her way to David's room. He hadn't come home yet, so she decided he wouldn't mind if she slept in his bed.

Nanea was drifting off to sleep when she heard quiet footsteps move down the hall.

The door creaked open. She sat up. "David?"

A familiar voice whispered back. "Nanea? What are you doing in here?"

It *was* David! "You're home!" She made her way to the door in the dark and threw herself at him.

"Yes, Monkey." He ruffled her hair.

Nanea didn't want to let go. She sucked David's Old Spice smell deep into her lungs. Then she coughed. He hadn't showered in a few days.

"Where were you? What were you doing?" she asked. "What did you see?"

"Slow down there, Monkey," David sat down on the bed. "One question at a time."

"Why were you gone so long?" Nanea asked impatiently.

She heard first one shoe and then another drop.

"I couldn't leave," he said. "Not with so many injured men counting on me."

"What do you mean?"

"I've spent the last three days delivering bottles of blood from the Red Cross and running them to the operating rooms." He paused. "And I thought it was hard doing sprints in PE." He was quiet for a moment before speaking again. "This one guy named Harold had a broken arm, but he still managed to pull his buddy Stan out from under a plane at Hickam Field. Stan was in pretty bad shape. The doctor said if I hadn't shown up with the blood when I did, he might not have made it."

"Were you scared?" Nanea asked.

"Sometimes," David admitted. "Listening to Harold describe what he saw at the airfield was scary. But I was glad I was able to help. I even got to meet Stan." David cleared his throat. "He's from Ohio. A real nice guy. Has a pesky little sister, like I do."

Nanea shivered. She hadn't been thinking about the people who had been hurt in the attacks. People like Harold and Stan. They had brothers and sisters and moms and dads who were far away and worried about them.

She leaned against David's shoulder. He could call her pesky all he wanted. She was that thankful he was home. "You did a lot, Kekoa," she said. He was named well. He really was a warrior.

"I wish I could have done more." David yawned deep and loud. "I'm fading, little Monkey. See you in the morning."

There was a thump, and Nanea realized David had fallen into bed. She felt around for the sheet to cover him up. He'd been taking care of others, and she was glad she could take care of him.

"Good night," she whispered. She felt light enough

to fly. David was home! Safe and sound.

Mom had been humming all morning. That's how happy she was.

"Will you help us look for Mele?" Nanea asked her brother. He had slept a long time and was eating breakfast while she ate lunch. "It's been four days, and we haven't found any sign of her."

"I wish I could, Monkey," David said, "but I have to report back to the hospital."

"I thought you would stay home for a while," she said.

He ruffled her hair. "There are still a lot of supplies to be delivered," he said. "And I want to see how Stan is doing."

Nanea frowned. She wanted David home. Weren't there other people who could work at the hospital? "Will you help me tomorrow?"

"I don't like to make promises I can't keep." He grinned his movie-star grin as he finished his meal. "Besides, you're going to find that goofy poi dog any minute. I just know it." He kissed Mom and was gone.

"I know it's hard for you to say good-bye to David when he just got home," Mom said. "But I'm proud of him for what he's doing."

"I know," Nanea sighed. "I am, too."

Mom smoothed her hands over her apron. "I'm just grateful that he's too young to be a soldier," she said under her breath.

❀

Nanea was glad to be outside. Since the attack, Mom had hardly let her leave the house, and she could only look for Mele if someone went with her. Today, Lily and Donna were coming along.

At the Sudas', Nanea straightened the pile of shoes on the porch while she waited for Lily. When she came out, Lily was holding a small rubber ball. "I know how much Mele loves balls. Maybe she'll hear it bouncing and come running."

Nanea thought that was a good idea. She and Lily walked to Donna's house, where their friend was waiting for them outside.

"I have a good feeling," Donna said, giving them each a piece of bubble gum. "Today is the day we find Mele. Look—I've got a secret weapon." Donna pulled something from her pocket. "Ta-da! A bone."

Nanea smiled. What would she do without her friends?

They hunted high and low without seeing one sign of Mele. No gray fur. No bright eyes. No waggy tail. Nanea felt utterly discouraged. And not just about Mele. Her neighborhood had always been so friendly and cheerful. Now the houses looked glum, with their windows framed by dark fabric or paper, ready to be pulled across for the nighttime blackout. A few windows had even been painted black! It was as if the attack had taken all the bright colors out of their island.

After she walked her friends home, Nanea wandered into her own backyard. Tutu and Mrs. Lin were leaning over the back fence, talking in hushed tones.

"I heard the Japanese are planning another attack next week," Mrs. Lin was saying.

Nanea stopped dead in her tracks. *Would they really do that?* she wondered.

"That's a rumor," Tutu said firmly, swatting at a mosquito. "It's best not to listen to them—or repeat them."

When Mrs. Lin saw Nanea, she changed the subject.

Nanea went inside, reminding herself that Tutu was very wise. If she said not to listen to rumors, Nanea was going to follow that advice. She just had to figure out how to tell the difference between a rumor and the truth.

Mary Lou and Iris sat on the sofa, talking quietly. Both of them had crumpled tissues in their laps, and their eyes were red from crying.

"What's wrong?" Nanea's heart pounded.

"My brother Al," Iris dabbed her eyes, "enlisted!"

"You mean joined the Army?" Nanea asked.

Iris turned her tissue around in her hand. "He says it's his duty."

"Dickie Evans joined, too," Mary Lou added. "And Puakea Bowman."

Nanea was confused. "But aren't they both still in high school?"

Mary Lou pulled her knees to her chest, wriggling her bare toes into the sofa cushion. "They're eighteen. That's all that matters."

"I'm proud of my brother," Iris sniffed, "but I don't want him to get hurt."

Nanea felt the same way about David.

"Come on." Iris tugged Mary Lou to her feet. "Let's go to my house. We can bake some cookies for Al and the other boys."

After they left, Nanea rummaged through the stack of newspapers on the coffee table. As she started reading, Tutu came inside and joined her.

"Oh my." Tutu pointed to a series of photos that showed the destruction in the harbor. Greasy snakes of smoke curled up from the USS *Arizona*, the *Oklahoma*, and the *Utah*, huge battleships that were now gone. "It says here that more than two thousand soldiers and sailors have been killed."

Nanea drew in her breath. "Why did they have to attack us?"

"The Japanese weren't attacking *us*, exactly," Tutu explained. "They were trying to destroy the battleships in the harbor and the fighter planes at the airfields."

Nanea was confused. "But why?"

"They don't want America to be able to fight back," said Tutu. She put her arm around Nanea. "War is a terrible thing. For both sides."

Nanea felt comforted by Tutu's warmth and the smell of her talcum powder. Before the bombing of

Pearl Harbor, Nanea wanted her 'ohana to stop treating her like a baby. Now she wished she could snuggle up in Tutu's lap and hear one of the lullabies her grandmother used to sing when Nanea was tiny.

They sat quietly for several minutes. "I hope Papa comes home soon," Nanea said.

"Your papa is doing important work," Tutu said. "He's repairing the damaged ships—getting the fleet ready to sail again."

Nanea was proud of Papa for helping, but he had important work to do at home, too. She needed to hear a Papa joke, to kiss a scratchy Papa cheek.

"So it's true." Tutu pulled the newspaper closer. "Governor Poindexter stepped down on December seventh. We're under martial law." She clucked her tongue. "That is one very big change."

"What's martial law?" Nanea asked.

"It means the military is in charge of everything. The fire department. The police. Even the governor's job will be given over to the military."

"Is that bad?" Nanea asked, tracing the flowers on Tutu's mu'umu'u.

Tutu sat quietly for a moment. "Well, what has

happened is very serious. I think President Roosevelt is trying to keep us safe. Perhaps that will be easier to do with the Army in charge." She crinkled the newspaper. "But it means a lot of new rules. They've closed the movie theaters. Many of the parks, too."

"All the fun things," Nanea muttered. She didn't think she liked this martial law. Besides, if the new people in charge felt like they had to make a bunch of rules, they didn't know much about Hawaii. People helped each other without being told. Even little kids could get along fine following one rule: aloha.

Tutu was still reading the paper. "There's a curfew now, too," she said.

"What's a curfew?"

"The time you must be home. No going out after nine o'clock at night . . . or eight o'clock if you're Japanese." Tutu batted at the paper. "That is not right. The curfew should be the same for everyone."

It seemed that people's outsides were suddenly more important than their insides. Uncle Fudge had been arrested because he looked like the enemy. But he was not the enemy. If the FBI had really known him, that would never have happened. Why should the

Japanese people on the island be treated differently?

Nanea saw something about schools near the bottom of the page. "Closed for at least one more month," she read aloud. All that time away from school was one more change that Nanea hadn't asked for. "What will I do until then?" she asked.

"How about the contest?" Tutu pointed to a small headline: Honolulu Helping Hands Contest extended to January fifteenth. "Now is certainly the time to lend a hand."

Nanea had forgotten all about the contest. "I guess so," she said. The change of deadline should have felt like good news. But Nanea's heart and head were filled with worries about the people she loved, her burned-up school, and her beautiful island. Those things mattered more than winning a bicycle.

KITTEN TROUBLE

⚉ CHAPTER 9 ⚉

he house was quiet after breakfast the next morning. Tutu and Tutu Kane went to check on Pono's Market. David went back to the hospital. Mary Lou went to the high school, which had been turned into an evacuation center for people whose homes had been damaged by the bombing. She and her friends were helping serve meals there. Nanea was finishing the dishes and was just about to go out and look for Mele when Mom bustled into the kitchen, pulling on a hat.

Nanea dried her hands on a towel. "Where are you going?" She wanted the family that was home to *stay* at home.

"Grandpop and Grandmom have to be worried sick," Mom explained. "We need to send a telegram to let them know we're all right." She slipped her pocketbook strap over her arm. "Come on, honey."

But we're not all right, Nanea thought. Instead, she said, "What about looking for Mele?"

"We can go after we send the telegram. I promise." Mom rested her palm against Nanea's cheek. "You can't stay home by yourself."

"But Mele—" Nanea started.

Mom didn't let her finish. "Are you going to wear shoes or go barefoot?" she asked.

"Shoes," Nanea said with a sigh. And she went to the front porch to get them.

"We've been in this line forever," Nanea grumbled at the Western Union office.

"There are a lot of people who need to send messages to their families," Mom said, adjusting her hat. "We just have to wait."

Nanea tried to be patient. First she had a contest with herself to see how long she could stand on one leg. Then she tried to think of as many words as she could that started with the letter M. But the first word that came to mind was Mele.

She couldn't help fidgeting. "I'm hot."

Mom sighed. "There's a patch of shade under that palm tree over there. Why don't you go sit for a bit?"

It was cooler in the shade. And also more interesting. Several posters were tacked to the tree. She had to stand on tiptoe to read them. "Need a car. Cheap. Call this number." "Apartment for rent." A small one read, "Lost cat. White with black stripes. Named Rover."

Nanea thought that was a funny name for a cat. Usually Rover was a dog's name. Did the cat chase balls? Chew on bones? Bark?

All those things made her think of Mele. Maybe she should make some lost dog signs. If they could help find Rover, they could help find Mele. Nanea was sure Lily and Donna would pitch in! And they could post them at the Portuguese bakery and at Mrs. Lin's shop and other places around the neighborhood. Nanea couldn't wait to get started. She ran into the telegraph office to tell Mom about her idea.

Mom had finally made it up to the front desk. "I'm almost done," she said to Nanea as she handed the telegraph form over to the man behind the desk.

"Mitchell Family, Beaverton Oregon," he read

aloud. "Got it." He squinted, counting the words. "This is over the ten-word maximum, so it'll cost more than the usual seventy-two cents." He gave Mom the total.

She fished a dollar bill and some coins out of her purse to pay. "Mahalo."

"We're awful busy," the man said, glancing at the calendar. "This won't likely arrive until tomorrow. December twelfth."

"We appreciate how hard you are working," Mom told the man. Nanea noticed that he had dark circles under his eyes.

"Around the clock the past few days," he said with a weary smile. "Aloha."

Nanea hurried Mom past the long line that stretched out of the Western Union office. From there to the bus stop, and then from the bus stop to home, Nanea eagerly explained her poster project.

"I think you've come up with a great idea, honey," Mom said. "Good thinking."

At home, Nanea raced through the front door and telephoned Donna. "Meet me at Lily's house. Important Kitten business!" Then she put some paper and crayons in her book bag and ran up the street.

She and Donna arrived at the same time. Aunt Betty answered their knock. "Come in, girls," she said.

"I have a great idea for finding Mele," Nanea announced. But then she hesitated. Lily was curled up on the sofa, and her eyes were puffy and red-rimmed. "Maybe now isn't a good time?" she asked.

Lily wiped her eyes. "No, I want to hear," she said.

Nanea pulled paper and crayons out of her bag while she explained about the lost dog poster.

"Keen idea!" Donna plopped down on the floor, chomping on her bubble gum as she began to draw.

Lily sat up and reached for the crayons. "I'll help, too."

Nanea smiled. "You two are true blue friends."

Each drawing of Mele looked a bit different. The ears on Donna's picture were a little too pointy, and Lily forgot to include the bit of white on Mele's shoulder, but anyone could tell the drawings were of Nanea's dog.

"Hey, where's your radio?" Donna asked Lily as she took a break from drawing to shake out her hand. "It's always right there by the sofa."

Lily paused as she reached for the gray crayon. "We

had to turn it in to the police."

"What for?" Donna asked.

"Is that another new rule?" Nanea sighed. She wondered if her family would have to give up their radio, too.

"Only for us." Lily set down the crayon.

"I don't understand," Donna said, sitting back on her heels. "Us?"

In a tiny voice, Lily answered, "Because we're Japanese."

"But you're loyal Americans!" Nanea said. "Your family's lived here forever!"

"I guess that doesn't count." Lily pushed her poster aside. "We also had to turn in our camera."

"That is nutty." Donna blew another bubble and popped it loudly.

A tear plopped on Lily's poster. "Last night, Gene came out of work and someone had written in soap on his windshield. It said, 'Go home, Jap.'"

Nanea gasped. "That's terrible."

"I'd like to find the person who wrote that and sock him in the nose." Donna made a fist with her hand. "Pow."

Lily laughed a little, even if it was a sad laugh. "You might have to sock a lot of people. It's not easy to be Japanese right now," she said. "I really wish Daddy was here."

"I know what you mean," Nanea said. "I don't know when Papa's coming home."

"Me either," Donna said. "My dad's been at the shipyard for four days."

Lily pushed her paper away. "It's not the same. Your dads weren't taken away." She ran to her room and slammed the door.

Donna and Nanea stared at each other.

Aunt Betty hurried in from the kitchen. "I'm sorry, girls," she said as she headed down the hall to Lily's room. "We're all so upset about Lily's father; it's difficult to know who to be angry at."

This war is wrecking everything, Nanea thought.

When Nanea got home from Lily's house, the kitchen countertops were covered with bread, lunch meat, and condiments. Mom was making sandwiches, and then passing them to Auntie Rose, who wrapped them in wax paper and added them to a tall stack.

"That's a lot of lunch," Nanea said.

"These are for the aid workers," Mom explained. "Firefighters, police officers, air raid wardens. Since so many restaurants and grocery stores are still closed, it's difficult for them to buy anything to eat. So we'll feed them. It's one way we can help."

"Come dip your paddle in," Auntie Rose said.

"Yes," Mom agreed. "Give us a hand."

Nanea was glad to help, but she wanted to tell Mom about what had happened at Lily's house. She needed some advice about making her friend feel better. But before she could say anything, Auntie Rose handed her the roll of wax paper.

"Take over for me, please, keiki. I'm going to call our neighborhood precinct."

Nanea was confused. "You're calling the police?"

Auntie Rose laughed. "Yes, but just to let them know there's food here. They'll make an announcement on their channel."

After Auntie Rose made the call, Mom turned up the volume on the radio. Ever since the commercial stations had gone off the air on Sunday, the Mitchells had kept their radio tuned to the police band for information. After a few minutes, Nanea heard their address announced.

It wasn't long before tired, hungry men in dirty clothes were knocking at their front door. Mom served them coffee as they helped themselves to sandwiches.

"I haven't eaten in two days," one firefighter said, taking a big bite. "You don't know how good this is!"

Nanea gave him two more sandwiches. "Have you seen my father, Richard Mitchell?" she asked. "He works at Pearl Harbor shipyard."

The firefighter shook his head. "My post is downtown. But don't you worry about your pop. I bet someone's taking care of him over there, too."

That made Nanea feel better. And maybe someone was giving Mele a scrap of food and a bowl of clean water. It was the way of the islands: *ho'okipa*, hospitality.

"Thanks, kiddo." The firefighter returned the empty coffee cup. "I better get back to it."

"Wait!" Nanea showed him one of the lost dog posters. "I'm trying to find my dog, Mele. Have you seen her?"

The firefighter studied the poster, and then shook his head. "I haven't. But I'll keep my eye out for her. Give me one of these and I'll put it up at the station house." He took the poster in one hand, then saluted Nanea with the other.

After that, Nanea made sure everyone got a lost dog poster with their sandwich. All the hungry workers assured her that Mele would return.

With her whole heart, she wanted to believe them, each and every one.

IN THE DARK

anea was curled up on the sofa, reading, when Mom announced that it was time to get ready for the blackout.

While Mom and Mary Lou pulled the blankets down over the windows, Nanea went around the house, turning out the few lights that were on. With each button she pushed, the house grew gloomier. And so did her spirits.

Handing out sandwiches all afternoon had kept her busy and had kept her mind off her sad feelings. But now that the workers were gone and the house was dark, her worries wriggled back in like geckos, over, under, and around. Nanea's finger rested on the last light switch. This would be the fifth pitch-black night. The fifth night of staying inside in the stuffy dark house instead of roller skating or playing tag or kick the can with the Kittens and other neighbor kids.

It was also the fifth night without Papa. It seemed like years since Nanea had sat on the porch with him, listening to the trilling crickets and the funny little quacks of the geckos. As their neighbors washed supper dishes, she and Papa would talk about their dreams, plan fishing trips, and tell jokes. The "before" night sky had been soft, twinkling with stars. This "after" nighttime was sharp and lonely.

David had shown her how to make a portable lantern by pounding holes into an old Crisco can with a nail and setting it upside down over a small candle. But even that tiny flicker of light had to be hidden from Mr. Lopez, the air raid warden. Nanea could use it only if she took it into a closet. It was tough for a girl used to running all over the neighborhood to crawl into such a tiny space. But it was the only way she could read, and reading helped make the long, dark nights go faster.

Mom lit the lantern candle and then set it in Nanea's closet hideout. Nanea curled up in a nest of pillows, opening to where she'd left off in *Mr. Popper's Penguins*. But tonight, not even the antics of those silly penguins could distract her.

In the living room, Tutu Kane started playing his ukulele. The notes of "Hawaii Aloha" tiptoed into Nanea's closet and into her lonely heart. She blew out the candle and went to join the others.

Nanea made her way over to her grandfather's chair, only bumping into the coffee table once. Tutu Kane finished "Hawaii Aloha" and then began "Mai Poina 'Oe Ia'u: Forget Me Not," softly singing the beautiful words in Hawaiian and then in English.

> *There's no other one I hold so dear*
> *Oh beloved of this heart of mine.*

The last time he'd sung this love song was at Nanea's cousin's wedding. All the aunties had cried.

"A love song can be about a place, too, can't it?" Nanea asked when her grandfather finished.

"Yes, you can love a place," Tutu Kane answered in the dark.

Nanea sighed. "I miss how everything was before Sunday."

"I miss our beloved Oahu, too," said Tutu Kane. A sad silence hung in the air.

"Shall we have some more music?" Tutu asked.

As Nanea felt her way over to the sofa by Mom, tears trickled down her face. She didn't bother to brush them away in the dark.

"Troubles seem bigger when you keep them to yourself," Mom whispered as Tutu Kane played "Do you want to talk?"

Nanea found Mom's hand and turned the wedding band around and around on Mom's finger. "It seems like the things I thought mattered—like winning the Helping Hands contest—don't anymore," Nanea said. "Not after everything that's happened. Everything's changed." She snuggled into Mom. "I want Papa to come home."

"I do, too," Mom said. "But we all have to make sacrifices to help win the war, and that means sharing Papa." Mom put her arm around Nanea. "Sometimes the best thing we can do is keep paddling our canoe, no matter what the waves around us are doing."

"So I should keep going with the contest?"

"That's for you to decide."

"There's something else." Nanea lowered her voice. "Lily got mad at me and Donna today. We said we knew what it was like not to have a dad around because our dads are off working. Lily said it wasn't the same thing at all."

"Poor Lily." Mom gave Nanea a squeeze. "And poor Nanea and Donna."

Tutu Kane sang with warmth; Tutu and Mary Lou hummed along.

Nanea gathered the courage to say aloud the words she'd been thinking since she left Lily's. "What if Lily doesn't want to be friends anymore? She was so . . . so . . . prickly! Like a pineapple top!"

Mom sighed. "Oh, I was poked so many times picking pineapples when I was young. And do you know what Tutu would do?"

Nanea shook her head. Then she remembered Mom couldn't see her in the dark. "No," she said.

"She would rub on a soothing ointment. Worked every time." Mom squeezed Nanea again. "I bet you can think of something to soothe Lily's prickles."

"But so many bad things have happened to her family," Nanea said. "Uncle Fudge is in jail, and the Army took away their radio and camera." Nanea told Mom what someone had written on Gene's car.

"That's terrible!" Mom exclaimed. "The Sudas are not the enemy. Hawaii is their home, and they would never do anything disloyal to America."

Nanea leaned into Mom. "I want to do something to help Lily."

"Keep being her friend. You'll find a way to help her." Mom patted Nanea's leg.

Nanea thought and thought. But, for once, she didn't have any good ideas.

Hellos and Good-byes

🐚 CHAPTER 11 🐚

anea sat at the kitchen table writing a letter while Mom and Tutu made dinner.

December 14, 1941
Dear Grandmom and Grandpop,
  It's been seven days since you-know-what,
and seven days since Papa's been home.
Everyone is busy helping with the war ef-
fort. Mary Lou's working at the evacuation
center. Mom's joined the Red Cross and is
organizing first aid classes. David is either
volunteering at the hospital or working at
the hotel, so he's hardly ever home. I helped
hand out sandwiches.

Nanea stopped writing. Handing out sandwiches

sounded unimportant compared to what everyone else was doing. She felt like the baby of the family all over again. She sighed and kept writing.

> *I go out looking for Mele every day. I never thought that dog would stay away one whole week. Tutu and Tutu Kane are still with us. We didn't have hula lessons yesterday, but Tutu says she wants to have class again next week, even if it's only me and Mary Lou. We need to rehearse for the Christmas program at the USO, though the show may be canceled. The Matson ship that brings the evergreen trees from Washington was turned back, and there are no lights down-town because of the blackouts.*

As she worked on the letter, Nanea heard a car in their driveway. It wasn't David. He was home for once, and he and Tutu Kane were in the backyard, digging a hole for a bomb shelter. That was another new rule. Every home had to have a place to take cover during air raid drills.

Before Nanea could get up from the table to see who had pulled in, the front door opened. Suddenly, someone was standing in the kitchen.

"Papa!" Nanea cried. "You're home!" She flung herself into his arms.

"Sunshine!" Papa caught her and rocked her in his arms. "Oh, I'm so glad to see you."

Papa put Nanea down and gave Mom a long hug. Tutu wiped her eyes with her apron. Mary Lou rushed in from the bedroom, and David and Tutu Kane hurried in from outside. Everyone was hugging everyone and talking all at once. It was wonderful.

"Is Mr. Hill home, too?" Nanea asked.

Papa nodded. "I dropped him off a few minutes ago."

Nanea had a million other questions. "Papa, did you—"

But Mom cut her off. "Give your father a moment," she said.

Papa kissed Nanea's cheek. "Let me get cleaned up," he said. "Then we can all talk."

Twenty minutes later, Nanea's whole family sat down for supper.

"We missed you," Nanea said, passing Papa a plate of grilled tuna.

"And I missed you. But there is a lot of work to do—debris to clean up, repairs to manage. We had to cut open a capsized ship to rescue some trapped sailors." Papa hesitated. "But the Navy doesn't want me talking much about all that."

Nanea heard a sadness in Papa's voice that had never been there before. There was a long pause as everyone began to eat.

"At least our whole family is together again," Mary Lou said.

Nanea frowned. "Except for Mele."

Papa put down his fork. "What happened?"

Nanea told him everything. "Do you think she'll come back, Papa?"

"Did I ever tell you about my old mutt, Rusty?"

"Lots of times," Nanea said.

"Did you know he once went missing for three whole months?"

"No." Nanea could hardly believe there was a Rusty story she hadn't heard.

"The goofy dog never would say where he'd got

off to," Papa chuckled. "But he showed up one day, right at suppertime, as if he'd only been gone a few minutes." Papa picked up his fork. "Dogs don't have the same sense of time we do. Mele will be back."

Nanea couldn't bear the thought of waiting three months to see her sweet little dog again.

After dinner, no one wanted to leave the table. Everyone kept talking, and Papa had seconds on dessert, but soon his eyes began to close.

"Your father needs to sleep," Mom said. "And we all have chores to do before the blackout. Mary Lou, you're in charge of dishes. David, get the windows covered. Nanea, finish your letter to your grandparents."

Nanea smiled as Mom ordered everyone about. Nanea kept smiling as she finished her letter. *"Here is the best news ever,"* Nanea wrote. *"Papa's home. Safe and sound."*

That night, as Nanea curled up on the couch, she felt like she was able to truly relax again. Papa was back, and he was like a coral reef protecting the family from fears and worries that might swim too close. She was so happy.

Nanea's eyes popped open. What about Lily?

Her father wasn't home yet. Would this be one more prickle between the Kittens?

When she awoke, Nanea instantly remembered: Papa was home! She jumped off the couch and raced into the kitchen. "Good morning!" she called out.

"Shh," Mom put a finger to her lips. "Your father's still sleeping." Nanea poured herself a glass of pineapple juice and sat down at the table.

Mom turned back to Tutu. "Richard left the shipyard just once in the last week," Mom said to Tutu. "It was at night, so he got a ticket for driving with his headlights on!"

Tutu shook her head. "That's one of the new rules," she said. "Car lights have to be dimmed during the blackouts. But when has Richard had time to paint over his headlights?"

"He's been working around the clock," Mom added.

Tutu took a sip of coffee. "Speaking of rules, the government wants to know what supplies are available on the island. All the grocery stores had to take inventory last week. Now your father and I need to do the same at the market. It will take a few days. "

"I'm sorry I can't help," Mom said. "I'll be at the Red Cross every day this week. Mary Lou's volunteering at the evacuation center, and David is at the hospital."

"I could help," Nanea offered.

Mom hesitated. "I don't know."

"I think it's a great idea," said Tutu. "Nanea can reach the cans and boxes that are down too low for me and Tutu Kane."

Nanea smiled. "I'm good at numbers, too," she said, hoping to convince her mom.

"Well . . ." Mom paused. "All right," she finally agreed.

Nanea nearly spilled her juice. A few weeks ago d asked to help in the market, and Mom had ght she was too young.

Good." Tutu nodded, picking up her coffee cup.

ll start tomorrow."

iddenly, Nanea had another idea. But she wanted ne to be a surprise. "Can I go outside?" she asked.

tay in the yard," Mom cautioned.

Outside, Nanea held her breath as she searched the sky for planes and black smoke. In the last week, it had become a habit to look up. She exhaled, relieved to see only calm clouds floating above.

In the garage, Nanea found two cans of paint on Papa's workbench, one gray and one black. She decided to paint each headlight a different color. She popped the lids off the cans with a screwdriver like Papa always did. She found two paintbrushes and got to work, thinking of how pleased Papa would be that she'd taken care of this for him. It was a little tricky working on the smooth, curved lights, but she was careful not to get any paint on the car.

Nanea heard whistling as the back door opened and Papa walked to the driveway. "Time for break—," Papa stopped when he saw what she was doing. He looked surprised.

"I didn't want you to get another ticket," Nanea explained. "And you needed your sleep."

Papa's face softened to a smile. "I know you meant well," he started. "But that's not how it's supposed to be done."

Nanea felt terrible. "I only wanted to help."

"I know that, Sunshine," Papa said.

Nanea sighed, waiting for him to remind her, once again, to "think before you act."

But he didn't. Instead, he went to the garage for a can of paint remover and some rags. "It won't take long to put this right."

Together they cleaned the paint off each headlight. Then Papa explained the proper way to do it. "The bottom half is supposed to be black, and the top half is supposed to be gray." He pressed a small piece of masking tape across the center of each light. "When the paint is dry, we'll take off the tape, and the light will shine through this space in the middle. Now, you paint the top and I'll paint the bottom. Then we'll paint the tail lights."

After they finished, they cleaned the brushes and tapped the lids back on the paint cans. "I'm starving!" Papa said. "I hope David left us some breakfast."

Back in the kitchen, Mom refilled Papa's coffee cup three times. Papa didn't say a word to the rest of the family about Nanea's mess-up.

"How many sandwiches do you want in your lunch?" Mom asked Papa.

"Lunch?" Nanea asked.

"I've got to get back, honey," Papa said.

"But you just came home!" Nanea pushed her plate away. "It's not fair!"

"Fair!" Mary Lou exclaimed. "Nothing has been fair since the war started."

"Everyone is being asked to do their part to help," Mom added.

Papa looked across the table at Nanea. "I think it'd be more unfair if I expected other people to do my work, don't you?"

Nanea kicked her chair leg, but she nodded. Then she went over to Papa and put her arms around his neck. She squeezed two times. Buddies forever. "When will you be back?" she whispered in his ear.

"In a couple more days." He kissed her cheek. "You'll be too busy to even notice I'm gone."

That would never, ever be true.

Starfish

🐚 CHAPTER 12 🐚

Twenty boxes of Corn Flakes," Nanea reported. She stretched her tired arms. "And two dozen bags of rice." Inventory was a big job! They had to make a list of everything in the shop and count it all. It would have been more fun to work in the market when there were customers, but Nanea was glad she could help her grandparents.

"Mahalo," Tutu Kane said, adding the date, December 17, 1941, to the last page of the inventory. "Once we turn in these counts, we can reopen. It'll be good to be busy with the market again."

"I wonder if there will be food shortages," Tutu said. "All the things that come from the mainland could be hard to get. There may even be rationing."

"I know what that is," Nanea said. "It's when people can only get a certain amount of something.

Like one pound of butter a month."

Tutu Kane untied his white work apron. "Pono's Market" was stitched on the front of it in red thread. "If food is rationed, we'll handle it with aloha."

"You're right. We'll take care of one another," Tutu said. "Like we've always done."

Tutu Kane hung his apron on a hook. "We should get this one home before her mother forgets what she looks like." He winked at Nanea.

"Wait," said Tutu, reaching for a cardboard box. "I want to pack some groceries for the Sudas. Let me find those crackers Tommy likes."

While Tutu gathered the groceries, Nanea straightened the poster of Mele in the front window.

"Do you think these will help find her?" she asked.

"Of course!" Tutu Kane answered. "Someone will certainly have news of that wandering dog of yours."

Over the last few days, Nanea had searched up and down the streets around Pono's Market. It was hard to imagine Mele running five miles from home to the Kaimuki neighborhood, but Nanea looked, just in case.

When Tutu had the groceries packed, she gave the box to Tutu Kane to load in the car. She gave Nanea a small bag of candy. "For all your hard work," she said.

Nanea held the sack on her lap as Tutu Kane drove them home. She still couldn't get used to the destruction throughout the city. Here and there were holes where houses once stood, and on every block, shop doors were covered with plywood. *Some of these doors might never reopen*, Nanea thought.

"Penny for your thoughts, keiki?" Tutu Kane asked. "It's not like you to be so quiet."

Nanea studied her grandfather's profile from the backseat. David had that same nose. "Do you think we'll ever go back to normal?" she asked. "I mean in Honolulu. On Oahu."

"I've been wondering about that myself," Tutu said.

"You know what I think?" Tutu Kane asked. "I think our island is a lot like a starfish. You know they can grow arms back, right?"

"Sure." Nanea wondered what starfish had to do with anything.

"But it doesn't happen overnight. It takes a year or more." Tutu Kane signaled to turn right, with his arm out the window, elbow bent, hand up. "Well, the attack

took a lot out of us. Like a starfish losing one of these."
Tutu Kane waggled the arm he was signaling with.
"But we're going to come back. It won't happen over-
night. But it *will* happen."

"Starfish." Nanea wanted her grandfather's words
to come true.

"Starfish," Tutu Kane repeated as he pulled up in
front of Nanea's house. "Here we are. Your home sweet
home!"

❀

The living room was full of Mary Lou's friends, all
winding balls of yarn or clicking away with knitting
needles. David wandered out of his room in his hotel
uniform. He was still working at the Royal Hawaiian,
even though there weren't many tourists left. He said
the Navy might be taking the hotel over as a place for
sailors to stay when they had R & R—rest and relax-
ation. But that hadn't happened yet.

Iris showed David an unfinished sock. "We're knitting our bit," she said.

"Good work." David's smile made Iris blush.

"Remember 'Purl' Harbor!" Mary Lou said as she
click-click-clicked her knitting needles.

"Are you going somewhere, too?" Nanea asked Mom. She had on her church hat and was pulling on a pair of gloves.

"Back to the Red Cross, remember?" She kissed Nanea's cheek. "Hello and good-bye!"

"Can I go with you?" Nanea asked.

"We're talking about starting a junior guild. But for now the work is for adults only." Mom picked up a stack of papers. "See you in a few hours."

Nanea plopped on the couch next to Iris.

"Want to knit?" Iris asked.

Nanea shook her head. "Tutu tried to teach me, and it was a disaster."

"How about winding the skeins into balls," Iris suggested. "That would be a huge help."

Nanea picked up a skein of yarn, pulled the loose end from the bottom, and started winding. Wind, wind, wind, wind, wind. War work was boring. She finished one ball and then went to her room.

On the nightstand was a framed photograph of Nanea and Lily on Uncle Fudge's sampan. But instead of making her happy, the photo made her sad. Uncle Fudge was still at the immigration station, and her friendship with Lily was still prickly. Nanea had called Lily every day since they'd made the lost dog posters, but Lily hadn't wanted to talk.

Nanea picked up the photo. It had been taken before Donna moved to the island. Nanea and Lily had spent the day with Uncle Fudge, and he had packed tasty bento boxes for lunch, tucking in Nanea's favorite, rice balls with pickled apricot. Afterward, he brought out a coffee can full of oatmeal cookies. "A sweet treat for sweet crew members," he'd said.

Lily and Nanea had eaten so many cookies that day! Aunt Betty and Mom would have had conniptions had they known. Nanea smiled. That memory was as sweet as those cookies.

Wait, Nanea thought. *Cookies!*

Maybe she couldn't get Uncle Fudge out of jail or change how some people were treating the Sudas. But she could make oatmeal cookies for Lily and Uncle Fudge. Then Lily would know how much Nanea cared about both of them.

PUKA

 hile Mary Lou transferred the last batch of cookies from the cookie sheet to the cooling rack, Nanea dialed a familiar number. Aunt Betty answered.

"Oh, do come over," she said. "Lily is excited to see you."

That news made Nanea's stomach jump around like a happy tree frog. Lily wanted to see her!

Mary Lou carried a small plate of warm cookies to her friends in the front room. The cookies tempted Nanea, but she didn't eat a single one. They were for Lily and Uncle Fudge. She cleaned up the kitchen while the cookies cooled, and then she packed them into a shoe box lined with wax paper.

She had only taken a few steps toward Lily's before a noise stopped her. It was a dog. Barking loudly. The commotion came from the Bradleys' house across the road, on the other end of the street from the Sudas.

Nanea ran to the edge of the yard. "Is anyone home?" None of the Bradleys answered, but the dog kept barking. Nanea raced around back. A pile of tools and shovels and buckets were stacked neatly next to the house, and there was a fresh hole in the corner of the yard. It looked like the one David and Tutu Kane had started digging in their own backyard for an air raid shelter.

But Nanea's attention was on *this* hole. The scrabbling noises were too loud for a gecko—even for an army of geckos! Nanea peered over the edge, her heart pounding with hope.

Two brown eyes peered back.

"Mele!" Nanea dropped the box of cookies and knelt down, so happy she began to cry. "Come, girl. Here!"

The hole was too deep for Mele to jump out, so she tried to clamber up to Nanea, pawing wildly at the dirt. The sides of the wall were too slick for her to get any traction.

"You need help," Nanea said. She ran to the

Bradleys' house and searched the pile of tools. There was a ladder! Nanea picked it up. *Oof.* It was heavy, but she dragged it across the yard. She set it on the ground and slid it into the hole. Mele was jumping and scrabbling frantically at the dirt walls, desperate to get out, so Nanea had to be careful not to knock her over with the ladder as she lowered it into the ground.

When the ladder hit the muddy bottom, Nanea tugged it into position to lean against the side of hole. She turned around and started climbing down. The ladder wobbled as Nanea put her weight on it. She moved her feet carefully, lowering herself step by step. "Easy, Mele," she said as Mele pawed at the ladder.

Two rungs from the bottom, Mele pounced on Nanea, licking her legs and making Nanea laugh.

"Oh, I'm glad to see you, too!" Nanea said as she stepped off the ladder. She threw her arms around Mele's neck and hugged her tight. "Pee-yew! You smell like you've rolled in a whole school of dead fish."

At her favorite word, Mele barked.

"Okay," Nanea said. "Let's get out of here." Holding tight to Mele, Nanea put one hand on the ladder and climbed slowly, rung by rung, to the top. She set

Mele on the ground, climbed the rest of the way out, and then pulled the ladder out behind her. She let it fall to the ground, and she plopped down next to it. Mele jumped into her lap. Nanea was hot and dirty and smelly and out of breath, but she had never been happier.

Mele ran to the shoe box, sniffing. "Are you hungry?" Nanea opened the package of cookies. "I bet Uncle Fudge wouldn't mind sharing a few with you." Mele ate the first cookie in one chomp. Then Nanea broke the next one into smaller pieces. "You need real food," she said, putting the lid on the box. She dragged the ladder back to where she'd found it, picked up Mele and the shoe box, and headed for home.

"Mary Lou!" Nanea called. "Look who I found!"

Mary Lou stepped out on the front porch. "Where have you been, you bad dog?"

"She's not bad!" Nanea said. "She fell into a hole in the Bradleys' backyard, and she couldn't get out."

Mary Lou's eyes were wide. "They just started digging that hole two days ago. I bet Mele was on her way home when she fell in." Mary Lou reached over to pet Mele, but then she stopped. "Woo-wee," she said, holding her nose. "Mele needs a bath before she can come inside." She looked Nanea up and down. "You do, too."

"Food first," Nanea said.

Mary Lou gave Mele water and then fixed a bowl of leftover rice and sausage and noodles. While Mele ate, Nanea filled an old washtub in the backyard. Nanea didn't think Mom would mind if she used the good bath soap this once.

After she was scrubbed clean and dry, a rose-scented Mele curled up on Nanea's pillow. "I'm sorry it took me so long to find you," Nanea said as she changed her dirty clothes. "I can't wait to tell Donna and Lily the good news."

Donna was thrilled when Nanea phoned. "I'm coming over to see her! Right after I finish helping Mom roll bandages for the Red Cross."

Next Nanea dialed Lily. Aunt Betty answered, and it took Lily a long time to come to the phone. "Oh, it's you," Lily said flatly. "I thought you were bringing something for my dad."

"I was," Nanea started. "Cookies. But—"

"That was *two hours* ago," Lily interrupted.

"I waited and waited. I thought you were my friend."

"I am!" Nanea tried to explain.

"I have to go." Lily hung up.

Nanea felt terrible. She went outside, Mele at her heels, and plunked down on the back porch. She rested her head in her hands.

"You found Mele!" Auntie Rose called over happily. "But that is one sad face. What is troubling my favorite neighbor?"

Nanea told her what had happened. "I didn't mean to let Lily down. But Mele needed me, too."

Auntie Rose nodded. "You were torn, trying to do kokua for two friends at the same time. You should go talk to Lily."

"She'll probably slam the door in my face." Nanea pulled her knees to her chest. "Maybe I'll go tomorrow. Or the next day."

"Best to swallow toads right away," Auntie Rose advised.

"Yuck," Nanea said. "Who would swallow a toad?"

Auntie Rose chuckled. "It means if something is difficult, do it and get it over with." She went back inside her cottage.

Mele rested her head on Nanea's lap. Nanea patted her, thinking. She made up her mind.

"Do you want to go for a walk?" Nanea asked.

Mele answered with a wagging tail. Nanea got the cookie package and, for the second time that day, started toward Lily's.

Lily was sweeping the porch when Nanea and Mele arrived. When she saw Mele, Lily broke into a smile. "You found her!"

Mele bounded up the stairs to give Lily a hello lick.

"That's why I wasn't here earlier," Nanea said, pausing on the bottom step. "She was trapped in a hole in the Bradleys' backyard. After I pulled her out, she was so hungry that I had to fix her some food. And she was so dirty that I had to give her a bath. That's what took so long." Nanea held out the package. "Here are the cookies I made. Oatmeal." She hoped Lily remembered that special fishing trip.

"Daddy loves oatmeal cookies." Lily came down the steps to take the package.

There was an awkward silence, and Nanea rubbed her hands nervously on her shorts. "I'm sorry," she finally said. "For everything."

"I'm sorry, too, for getting so mad." Lily sat down on a step and started scratching Mele's left ear. Nanea sat down and started scratching Mele's right one. Mele thumped her tail happily.

"I'm glad you found Mele, really I am." Lily sighed. "But it makes it harder, too."

Nanea cocked her head. "I don't understand."

"You've got your whole family back together now. Mine still has a *puka* in it. A big hole." She turned her face away.

"I know you're worried about your dad," Nanea began. "And I know cookies won't make that worry go away." She chewed on her lip, not sure what to say next. "Tutu says that troubles are like a big pail of water. Too heavy to carry alone."

Lily pressed her face into Mele's fur before looking over at Nanea. "Thanks for the cookies," she said. "And thanks for caring about me."

Donna came tearing up the street, calling Mele's name. Mele bounded off the steps to meet her, sniffing at the paper sack in Donna's hand. "Your favorite kind of crack seed, Lily!" Donna called joyfully, waving the bag of dried fruits. "Plums!"

She squeezed on the steps between Lily and Nanea, opening the sack. The girls ate until they were sticky messes, and when the last of the crack seed was gone, Donna tore the paper sack into three pieces and they chewed on those to get the very last of the sweetness of the preserved plums.

"Tutu is right," Lily said. "My pail of water doesn't feel as heavy with you two here."

"What pail of water?" asked Donna, looking around.

Nanea and Lily laughed. "We'll tell you later," Nanea said. "For now, let's go get washed up."

DECK THE HALLS

he calendar said December 24, but no one would know it by looking at the city of Honolulu. There were no Christmas trees in any of the houses. The bright holiday lights that usually invited shoppers into downtown stores had gone dark. Curfews kept nighttime carolers from their door-to-door concerts. And without school, there was no Christmas program at Lunalilo Elementary. This year, Nanea's class was supposed to have sung "Santa's Hula," about Santa in his red canoe.

Now that Mele was home, Nanea had been able to find some of her Christmas spirit again. She'd spent the last week making gifts, and today she taped the "Keep Out: Elves at Work" sign to her bedroom door one last time so that she could wrap the presents. She tied yarn around the last package and then stashed them all under her bed. "It's almost Christmas," Nanea said to Mele, who was curled up on her pillow.

Nanea wandered out to the kitchen, where Mom, Mary Lou, and Tutu were baking cookies. From the window Nanea could see Papa, David, and Tutu Kane finishing the air raid shelter in the backyard. Nanea reached for a cookie, but Mary Lou stopped her.

"These are for the soldiers who are spending Christmas in the hospital," Mary Lou informed her matter-of-factly.

"I think we can spare one cookie." Mom smiled at Nanea.

"Well, we need to do all we can to improve the soldiers' morale," said Mary Lou.

Nanea put the cookie down. "What about *our* morale? Don't ordinary people need their spirits lifted, too?"

Tutu smiled. "Of course we do. But we want to cheer up the soldiers who can't be home this Christmas."

Nanea made a decision. *I am going to cheer up my own 'ohana!* she told herself. She ran outside, Mele at her heels. They needed a Christmas tree, and there had to be *something* out there she could she use. A palm branch had fallen onto the front porch. Nanea dragged it into the living room. Then she rummaged around for some thumbtacks. All she could find were some rusty brass ones.

Nanea poked her head into the kitchen. "Mary Lou, can I use your fingernail polish?"

"You're too young to paint your fingernails," Mom said before Mary Lou could answer.

"It's not for my nails," Nanea explained. "It's for a Christmas project."

Mom stirred coconut flakes into a bowl of cookie dough. "That's all right then."

A quick coat of red fingernail polish changed the rusty thumbtacks into something fresh and festive. They looked like little berries poking out from behind the palm fronds.

David came in from outside. "What have you got going there?" he asked.

"Our tree," Nanea said. "What do you think?"

"What about a star for the top?" David asked.

Nanea pursed her lips. "I haven't figured that out yet. But I'm going to string it with paper leis."

"What are you going to string with paper leis?" Mary Lou asked, coming in from the kitchen. "A tree!" she exclaimed. "Let me help!" She ran for scissors and paper.

David went back outside, and Nanea and Mary Lou started making tiny leis. They were hanging the garland when David returned with Papa and Tutu Kane.

"Ta-da!" David held up a star, cut out of a tin can and pounded flat.

Papa hung it on the top of the palm branch tree. "David said there was a Christmas tree in the house, and I almost didn't believe him. Nice job, Nanea."

"What a good reminder that we can make our own Christmas spirit," said Tutu Kane.

"Best tree ever," David pronounced.

Mary Lou placed one of the extra paper leis around Nanea's neck. "Good idea, little sis," she said. "Now we're ready for Christmas."

That night, after the windows were covered, the whole family sang Christmas carols in the dark accompanied by Tutu Kane and David on their ukuleles. Even Mele joined in, howling along to "Santa's Hula."

"Wake up, sleepyhead!" Nanea called to Mary Lou. "It's Christmas!" For once, her big sister didn't grumble that it was too early.

Breakfast was a feast with all of Nanea's favorites—coconut pancakes and fresh papaya and Portuguese sausage! When everyone's bellies were full of delicious things—Nanea shared her last bite of malasada with Mele—they moved to the living room.

When she was younger, Nanea couldn't wait to open her presents. Now, she could hardly wait for the others to open the gifts she'd made.

Nanea had stitched several small drawstring pouches and embroidered a special design on each one. Mom opened her pouch first. "Oh, it's so pretty!" she said.

"The heart is because I love you so much," Nanea told her.

"And I got the music notes because of all my records," Mary Lou guessed. "This will be perfect to hold my lipstick."

"A bird of paradise!" Tutu exclaimed when she unwrapped her pouch.

"Because it's full of joy, like you," Nanea said.

"Thank you, keiki." Tutu blew her a kiss. "This is a treasure."

"Is it my turn?" Papa loved presents as much as Nanea did. "Well, look at this! A book about us going fishing!"

"See," Nanea moved closer. "There you are, catching the biggest fish."

Papa laughed. "That would be a change of pace."

"Maybe we can go fishing next week," she said.

"I would love to." Papa paged through the book Nanea had made. "But I don't get another day off until January sixteenth. I know that's a long wait, but I promise to take you then."

"Deal!" Nanea threw her arms around his neck, squeezing two times. "We'll catch lots of fish, no matter when we get to go."

"That is a very grown-up attitude." Mom smiled.

"Can I open my present now?" David asked.

Nanea had made David a book, too, and each page showed him doing something he loved—surfing, playing the ukulele, driving his jalopy. But Nanea had also drawn a little monkey in each scene.

"Ah," David said. "So I don't forget that my little Monkey is always with me." He ruffled Nanea's hair.

Tutu Kane examined his book very slowly. "This brings back many good memories," he said, smiling at the picture Nanea had drawn of him gathering wild tomatoes.

Nanea had a small pile of gifts to open. The first one was a new school dress Mom had sewn. "I hope I get to wear this soon!" Nanea said. Her gift from Mary Lou was a metal barrette with Nanea's name engraved on it. Nanea grinned. Her sister was still trying to fix her hair!

Tutu Kane and Tutu gave her a girl-sized white work apron. Nanea's eyes sparkled when she saw that Tutu had stitched "Pono's Market" on the front in red thread so it looked just like the aprons she and Tutu Kane wore in the shop.

"You were such a big help during inventory," Tutu said.

Tutu Kane nodded. "We hope you'll come back and work with us again."

Nanea slipped the apron on over her head. "Of course I will!" she replied happily.

Mele sniffed at the copy of *The Mystery of the Brass Bound Trunk* that was David's gift to Nanea. "I know you're crazy about those Nancy Drew books," he said. "But I didn't realize Mele was!"

The last gift was from Papa, who handed small packages to Nanea, Mom, and Mary Lou. "For my girls," he said.

Inside were delicate pins. "Oh!" Mom exclaimed. "How clever!" The pins said "Remember Pearl Harbor," but instead of the word *pearl*, there was a small pearl gem.

Nanea pinned hers to her dress right away. "Thank you, Papa." She wrapped her arms around Mele, studying each face around the room. The war had shaken up so many things. But it couldn't shake her family's love for one another.

At that moment the doorbell rang.

"Who on earth?" Mom muttered.

Papa opened the front door and gave a shout. "Fudge!"

The rest of the Suda family crowded inside.

"You're back!" Mom kept patting Uncle Fudge's arm as if she couldn't believe he was real.

Nanea ran to Lily. "Your daddy's home! I'm so happy for you!"

Tutu and Mom served coffee and coconut cake while Uncle Fudge talked story, with Tommy glued to his lap.

"Thank you for taking such good care of my family." He wrapped his arm around Aunt Betty.

"You're our family, too." Mom sniffled. Papa handed her his handkerchief.

"How did you get out?" David asked.

"Most of the men arrested were doctors, priests, teachers. Not fishermen." Uncle Fudge shrugged. "I guess the government had a plan to arrest all the community leaders if we went to war with Japan. To make it harder for the rest of us to organize or something." Uncle Fudge held up his hands, a look of bewilderment on his face.

"There was a Fumihiro Suda on the list," Gene said. "They thought that was Dad."

"As if any of the Japanese community leaders would be spies," Papa said.

"Fear makes people think and do foolish things," Tutu Kane said.

Uncle Fudge nodded his agreement. "My lawyer—the one you called for me, May—" he pointed to Mom. "He convinced the FBI they had the wrong Suda. And luckily, they're not going to arrest the other Suda."

"Which we're very thankful for." Aunt Betty patted Uncle Fudge's arm.

Mom sighed. "Well, we are thankful *you're* home."

A cloud passed over Uncle Fudge's face. "I never left the immigration station, but many others were sent to the internment camp on Sand Island." He shook his head. "I heard it's really bad there."

The room grew so quiet that Nanea could hear the kitchen wall clock ticking from the other room.

"One at a time," Tutu said softly.

"What?" Nanea asked.

"It's hard to gather the whole crop of mangoes at once," Tutu said. "You must harvest them one at a time. We will work to reclaim our neighbors the same way. One at a time."

Uncle Fudge lifted his glasses to wipe his eyes. Nanea glanced around. All the adults were wiping their eyes.

"How about more cake?" Mom asked.

"No, thank you," said Aunt Betty. "We should get home."

Tommy rode piggyback, while Lily held tight to her father's hand. Aunt Betty tucked her arm through Gene's.

"*Mele Kalikimaka!*" Nanea called as the family headed up the street. "Merry Christmas!"

It truly was the best Christmas ever. Because, finally, there were no more pukas in their family.

DOGGONE IT

ele whined and paced as Nanea got ready. "I'm sorry, Mele," Nanea explained. "But this isn't hula class. It's a USO performance. No dogs allowed."

"I'm a little nervous," Mary Lou confessed as she stood in front of the mirror fixing her hair. "This is our first show in over a month."

Nanea nodded. "I'm still sad that the Christmas dance was canceled."

"Me, too," Mary Lou agreed. "It seems odd to be doing a New Year's Eve performance at two o'clock in the afternoon, but that's the only way to make sure everyone's home in time for curfew." She placed one last bobby pin in her hair. "There. Are you about ready?"

"Almost!" Nanea answered. She removed her

holoku from a hanger and began to fold it. This was the
first time she was going to dance in the floor-length
gown with its ruffled train. Even if it was a hand-me-
down from Mary Lou, wearing it would still make
Nanea feel grown-up. She tucked the long train in on
itself as Mom had taught her, and then carefully placed
it on top of the implements in her 'eke hula. As soon as
she turned away, Mele tried to climb in the basket!

"No, Mele!" Nanea moved her basket. "I don't want
you to wrinkle my costume!"

Mary Lou shook her head. "What is wrong with
that dog?"

"I don't know." Nanea threw up her hands.
"Maybe it's all the firecrackers for New Year's." Some
of their neighbors had started lighting them earlier
in the day. "She's become skittish about loud noises."
Nanea reached under her bed and brought out one of
Mele's favorite balls. "Play with this. That should calm
you down."

But Mele didn't play. She flopped onto the floor,
panting, looking up at Nanea with sad brown eyes.

"Mele seems pretty upset," Mary Lou said. "I think
she knows you're leaving, and she wants to go, too.

"Maybe Auntie Rose would watch her," Nanea said. Ever since she had rescued Mele from the hole, the dog had stuck to her like a burr.

Auntie Rose was happy to keep an eye on Mele. "She can help me in my Victory Garden." Auntie Rose laughed. "I know Mele is good at digging holes!"

Nanea thanked Auntie Rose and then hurried to the car. At the USO Hall, Nanea changed quickly and then found Tutu backstage with the instruments.

All the dancers and musicians were either in the changing room getting ready or in the lobby setting up the refreshments they would serve after the performance. Nanea was glad to have a moment alone with her grandmother.

"Tutu," she began, shifting a pointed toe left to right.

Tutu straightened Nanea's *lei po'o*, which had slid forward on her head. "What is it, keiki?"

"It's the rising moon movement," she confessed. "I've been having a hard time with it.

Tutu pointed to her heart. "Hula is as much here as it is in the hands and feet." She smiled. "You've seen a moonrise, haven't you?"

Nanea nodded. Her favorite moonrise memory was from the year before. Papa had taken the Three Kittens camping and the girls had stayed up late.

"Place that moment in your heart," Tutu encouraged.

Nanea closed her eyes and remembered watching the milky moon take its place in the sky.

"Now, dance," Tutu whispered.

That moonrise memory started as a pearl of sweet warmth inside Nanea. Then it grew and grew, spreading to her shoulders, her elbows, her wrists, her fingers. She opened her eyes and tried the step.

"Lovely." Tutu hummed and began dancing with Nanea. Two small arms and two solid arms skimmed gracefully through the air, like delicate birds leaving tree branches to soar through the clouds.

When their dance ended, Tutu smiled. "You are a good *haumana*," she said.

"I'm a good student because I have the best teacher," Nanea replied. She gave Tutu a big hug.

The emcee arrived onstage. "There's a full house today," he told Tutu, gesturing to the other side of the curtain. "We'll start in five minutes," he said.

"Mahalo," Tutu said. "Nanea, would you gather the others?"

When all the dancers were waiting in the wings, a shot of nervousness fizzed in Nanea's stomach. She took a deep breath knowing the butterflies would go away when she started to dance.

Tutu gracefully stepped out from behind the curtain, up to the big microphone. "Aloha," she said. She introduced the hula studio, the chanters, and the musicians. "The hula is pleasing because of the kumu hula, the chanters, singers, musicians, and dancers all working together." She opened her arms as if gathering up the entire audience. "I hope you enjoy our dances," she said.

The youngest dancers performed first. They sometimes forgot what they were supposed to do, but the men in uniform—some of them wearing silly hats for New Year's Eve—clapped anyway.

Nanea helped the littles off the stage, the butterflies in her stomach multiplying. Her group was next.

"Smile," Tutu encouraged gently. Her warm voice relaxed Nanea. She found her place on the stage with the other girls and raised her arms, keeping her hands soft and elbows up. The music began. Nanea kept her eyes on her hands as they swept left and right while her feet moved left, right, forward, back. In a few more beats, it would be time for the moonrise motion. Nanea breathed deeply, drawing her memory into her heart. She danced just as she had with Tutu.

As the musicians played the final notes of the song, Nanea and the other girls pointed their right feet forward, reached their arms out, hands together, over their toes and bowed.

"That was the best you've ever danced," Mary Lou said when Nanea came off the stage. "It was beautiful."

Nanea saw Tutu smiling at her. Nanea smiled back, feeling lighter than she had in a long time.

After the performance, Nanea helped serve refreshments. She was just about to hand a cup of punch to a soldier wearing an arm sling when she heard a huge commotion.

"Stop! Stop!" someone's voice cried out.

Nanea turned to see a furry blur heading right at her. It knocked the cup from her hands, and punch went flying all over the soldier. "Mele! What are you doing here?" Nanea asked with astonishment as Mele bounded around her feet. "Why aren't you at Auntie Rose's?"

In answer, Auntie Rose came puffing into the room. "Someone set off firecrackers, and Mele got scared. She ran and ran. I think she was looking for you." Auntie Rose bent over, trying to catch her breath.

"Here's a seat, ma'am," the soggy soldier said, pulling up a chair with his good arm.

"And here's some punch." Mary Lou gave Auntie Rose something to drink.

"Your uniform," Nanea said to the soldier as she started wiping off his sleeve.

He laughed. "No harm done." He bent down so he was eye level with Mele. "Would she mind if I petted her?"

Mele's tail was wagging and her tongue was hanging out. "Mele looks pretty happy about that idea," said Nanea.

"Mele, huh?" The soldier scratched the spot right behind Mele's ears. "My name's Tennessee," he said. "Well, that's what my friends call me. To Uncle Sam, I'm Private First Class Ronald Paul." Mele flopped on her back so Tennessee could rub her stomach.

"She looks like my mutt, Champ," said another soldier.

"Look at that tail wag!" said another.

Nanea looked around. Mele was surrounded by men in uniform, as popular as a movie starlet.

Tennessee gave someone else a turn to pet Mele. "I miss my Blue something awful. Best hound dog in my hometown," he said.

"I'm sorry again about your uniform," Nanea said. She could hardly see Mele, with all the soldiers gathered around her. Nanea could tell they were all happy that Mele had joined the party.

Tennessee saluted Nanea. "Thanks to you, this is the best *doggone* New Year's Eve party ever." He winked. "But next time, I think I'll drink the punch instead of wear it."

Absolutely Essential

week after the USO show, Nanea opened her front door to the other two Kittens. "Perfect timing. There's fresh guava bread."

"No thanks." Donna kicked off her shoes. "I'm not hungry."

Nanea stared. Donna had never turned down a sweet treat.

"Can we go in your room?" she asked instead.

In Nanea's room, Donna started to sit on the bed.

"Wait, wait, wait!" Nanea hurried over. "We can't sit on the quilt. That would be disrespectful to Tutu and all the work she put into making this. See all those tiny stitches?" She traced around the turquoise flower appliques, bright like the ocean against the quilt's white background.

"Help me pull the quilt off first," she said.

After they moved the quilt, the Three Kittens sprawled on top of the sheets, and Mele took her place on Nanea's pillow. Donna sat quietly, running her hand over and over Mele's back.

Nanea realized that Donna wasn't chewing gum. "Are you okay?"

Donna opened her mouth to say something, then closed it again. She shook her head, and a teardrop plopped on Mele's fur.

"Tell us!" Nanea scooted closer. Lily did, too.

"Nonessential civilians have to leave," Donna said sadly.

"Who?" Nanea blinked.

"People like me and Mom," Donna said. "Wives and children of military personnel and civilian workers. People who don't have jobs and who aren't helping the war effort." Donna swiped at her cheek. "The Army says we're not necessary. That it'll be easier to feed and protect the island with fewer people. So we have to leave."

Nanea felt like she'd been slapped by a cold wave. "You *are* necessary!" she insisted. "You're essential!"

Donna shook her head. "I don't have a job, like

Dad, working in the shipyard, repairing the ships. Neither does Mom."

"But you're the third Kitten," Nanea protested. "That's a very important job!"

Mele had rolled onto her back, and Donna rubbed her tummy. "Not to the Army," she said.

"So you and your mom have to leave but your father doesn't?" Lily asked.

"That's right." Donna's tears overflowed at that answer.

"Wait a second." Nanea held up a hand. "This is probably another of those rumors."

Lily nodded in agreement. "Like when someone said that clothing store ad was full of clues for Japanese spies," she said.

"Right." Nanea slapped her hands on her thighs. "And that wasn't true."

"Or that arrows were cut in the cane fields to guide the Japanese Zeros," Lily added.

"Also not true." Nanea leaned forward. "This is the same thing. A rumor. So let's not borrow trouble." Nanea tried to sound confident, but she felt uncertain.

"I don't know." Donna bit her bottom lip.

Mele whined. "She needs to go out," Nanea said.

All three girls went to the backyard with Mele. Across the way, Auntie Rose was bent over a low tub.

"What are you doing?" asked Lily.

"Is that dye?" Donna asked.

Auntie Rose stood up and pressed her hands to the small of her back. "Now that the tourists have stopped coming, we lei sellers don't have any customers. But Uncle Sam has decided to use our sewing skills for making camouflage netting." She smiled proudly. "Now we are as busy as ever."

"What does the government want with camouflage nets?" Donna asked.

"They'll use them to cover buildings and equipment and even soldiers," Auntie Rose explained. "That way, enemy planes can't see them from the air."

Camouflage nets are essential, Nanea thought, *but my friend isn't?* Suddenly, Nanea had an idea. "Can we help?" she asked Auntie Rose.

Donna and Lily gave her funny looks. But Nanea didn't care. If it wasn't a rumor—if nonessential civilians had to leave—then she had a plan. As long as Donna *did* something essential, she would *be* essential.

The government would have to let her stay!

Auntie Rose handed each girl a stout stirring stick. "Be careful not to get any of the dye on your clothes," she said. "Or yourselves!"

Nanea's tub was olive green. She stirred the murky water in a figure-eight pattern. Donna stirred brown, and Lily black. They stirred and stirred and stirred.

"My arms are getting tired," Lily grumbled.

Donna groaned. "How much longer?"

"Keep going!" Nanea encouraged, even though her arms were tired, too.

"What are you so cheerful about?" Donna asked. "You're even whistling!"

Nanea didn't want to give her plan away. It would be a big surprise for Donna and Lily. "I'm just happy to be dipping my paddle in," she said.

Auntie Rose checked on their progress. "Looks good," she said. "I'll take over from here."

She carefully fished out the wet fabric strips, hanging them on shrubs around her yard so they could dry.

"One more step," she said. "Come, keep me company." Settling in a big wicker chair on her lanai, she began to tear lengths of dry fabric into strips, and then the strips into smaller bits. "We weave these strips into the netting," she explained.

"Can we help tear, too?" Nanea asked.

"Sure." Auntie Rose tossed them each a handful of fabric.

"This is easier than stirring," Lily said, ripping a strip of fabric in half.

"It's as easy as chewing gum," Donna added.

Nanea was so happy to be essential that she tore the pieces as fast as she could. "Oops!" She held a tiny scrap. "This one's too small. I'd better throw it away."

Auntie Rose stopped her. "Good nets are made with lots of different fabric scraps. All shapes. All sizes. No piece is too small."

Nanea's heart fluttered with joy. No piece was too small. That meant no helper was too small. Soon, the Army would see that all the Kittens were essential to the war effort. Especially Donna!

ANYTHING FOR A FRIEND

 ime to go," Mom called the next morning. Nanea closed her Nancy Drew book and waggled her fingers at Mele. "We're getting fingerprinted! I'll be back soon." Nanea shut Mele in the bedroom so the dog wouldn't come looking for her again. Then she hurried outside to David's car.

Nanea joined Mary Lou in the backseat. "I think it's going to be nifty to have an identification card to carry around. Kind of like the one I used to have for the Dick Tracy fan club. Only more grown up."

"That's one way to think about it, Monkey." David shifted gears. "But I wonder why ID cards are only required here in the Territory."

"You don't have to get an ID card if you live on the mainland?" Mary Lou asked.

David shook his head. "Nope."

"I'm sure there's a good reason," Mom said.

Nanea sighed. During war, it seemed especially important to follow the rules. And now there were so many new rules: when to be home, when to turn the lights out, even when to shop.

At the processing station, they went to the end of a long line. Nanea was trying to get used to such lines. They were everywhere: at the market, at the bank, at the post office. David found a friend to talk to while Mary Lou took a seat against the wall and pulled out the olive green muffler she was working on. Lately, she'd been so busy knitting that a layer of dust had settled on her record player.

Mom took a notepad from her pocketbook. "I need to talk to Mrs. Lin when we get home," she said, adding to her to-do list.

That will be a long conversation, Nanea thought. Mrs. Lin was very chatty! "What about?" Nanea asked.

"Now that we're trained first aid instructors, we want to do a class for the mothers in our neighborhoods. But there's a problem."

"Our house isn't big enough?" Nanea followed Mom as the line moved up.

"Well, that's true." Mom straightened her hat. "We're having the class in the high school cafeteria. No, the problem is child care."

"You mean someone to babysit?" Nanea asked. "Is that an essential job?"

Mom tilted her head. "Well, yes, I guess you could say that."

"The Kittens can do it," Nanea offered.

"There'll be around twenty youngsters," Mom said. "Too many for three girls."

"Well, we could get some other friends to help," Nanea suggested.

"What a fine idea!" Mom said.

"I'll ask some of the girls from my class," Nanea said. "I'm sure they'll all say yes."

"Wonderful." Mom shuffled forward with the line. "The class is set for next Friday, January sixteenth."

Nanea stopped. "Oh, no! Does it *have* to be that day?"

Mom nodded. "We've already made the arrangements with the school. What's wrong?"

"That's my fishing day with Papa," Nanea said. She had no idea when he would have another day off.

Mom made a sympathetic face. "You don't *have* to babysit," she said. "Go fishing with your dad."

"But you said everyone has to do their part for the war," Nanea pointed out.

Mom squeezed Nanea's shoulder. "You'll have other chances to help with the war effort."

Right now, Nanea's biggest war effort was keeping Donna in Hawaii. This seemed like the perfect chance to show how essential Donna was. "I think this is one sacrifice I should make," she decided. She would do anything to keep the Kittens together. She swallowed hard. "I'll tell Papa I can't go."

Mom put her arm around Nanea. "I'm proud of you. Maybe Papa will get another day off sooner than we think," she said hopefully. "Oh, it looks like it's our turn." She called Mary Lou and David, and the four of them stepped up to a desk.

The man behind the desk asked Mom some questions. Then the other members of Nanea's family got fingerprinted.

"Now I just need your index and middle finger," the man said to Nanea. He helped her press the fingers of her right hand, one at a time, to the inkpad and then on the card. Then he repeated the steps with her left hand. And that was it.

"Here you are," he said a few minutes later when he handed Mom the ID cards. "Next!"

A week later, Nanea realized that there was a problem. She was supposed to take the card everywhere, but she didn't carry a purse like her mother and sister, or a wallet like David and Papa.

"I'm going to lose it, I know it," she told David. They were in the living room, playing gin rummy.

"Eddie's little sister punched a hole in hers and wears it on a string around her neck," David said.

"It could still fall off." Nanea chewed on a fingernail. "Maybe I could get an ID bracelet, like Donna." Donna's new bracelet sparkled like diamonds around her wrist, accented by a shining silver charm engraved with all her information on it. "Only five dollars at Engholm's Jewelers."

Mom was folding laundry. "No bracelets in the budget," she said without looking up.

"They have cheaper ones," Nanea quickly added.

"Gin." David placed his card on the discard pile.

"Sorry, honey," Mom said. "Maybe you could make something."

Nanea slowly folded up her hand of cards, thinking. She'd made those fabric pouches for Christmas gifts. Why not make one for her identification card? With the drawstring, she could wear the pouch around her neck or at her belt.

"Very clever," Mom said when Nanea explained her idea. "It's like we said during the Depression: Use it up, wear it out, make it do, or do without!"

"My sister, the genius," added David.

Nanea got Mom's scrap bag and started sorting through the material. After she picked out a piece for her ID pouch, she had a great idea. She had been wondering how she and her friends would entertain the children they'd be babysitting. A craft project was just the ticket!

Nanea flipped through one of Mom's pattern books and found instructions for Simple Stuffed Animals. "Mom, may I use more of these scraps?"

"Take as many as you need," Mom answered.

Nanea made a supply list. Then she called each girl

to explain the craft project. Whatever each girl offered to bring, Nanea made a note on the supply list. When the calls were finished, Nanea knew they had everything they needed: fabric, buttons, yarn, cotton batts for stuffing, safety scissors, glue, and glitter.

"Tomorrow is going to be perfect!" Nanea said. She didn't think she'd be able to sleep that night. She was too excited to be doing something to prove that Donna was essential to the war effort.

NANEA IN CHARGE

On Friday, Mrs. Lin welcomed the girls to the cafeteria. "We'll be teaching in the room across the hall, and you'll have this nice big space for all the children."

"We'll set up over here," Nanea said. "I made name tags to safety-pin to the children's clothes, and I brought newspapers to line the tables."

"You've certainly thought of everything, Nanea!" Mrs. Lin said as Donna and Lily began unpacking the supplies.

Nanea smiled at the compliment. "All we need are the kids!"

When the children arrived, Lily, Makana, and Judy helped them with their name tags. Patricia, Alani, and Bernice helped the kids find seats, while Donna, Linda, and Debby finished setting out all the craft supplies.

"This is going to be fun," Nanea said.

"Fun." Bernice rubbed her leg. "If you like being kicked in the shin."

"It was probably an accident," Nanea said.

With each new arrival, the noise level grew. Finally, when all the children were seated, Nanea said, "Aloha, everyone!" She had to shout to be heard. "We have such a fun morning planned."

"Where are the snacks?" a scruffy boy asked. His name tag said "Lewis."

Bernice leaned toward Nanea. "He's the kicker," she whispered.

The children did not sit quietly waiting for instructions as Nanea had imagined. Instead, they started grabbing at the scissors and glue.

"Wait, wait!" Nanea called. But no one waited. No one could hear her over the clamor.

Alani put her fingers to her mouth and whistled. The noise startled everyone. Even Nanea.

"Thank you, Alani." Nanea tried to imitate her teacher, Miss Smith. "Now, you're going to start with a large scrap of fabric—not yet! Listen first!" It was too late. Children were already taking fabric scraps.

"I wanted that one!" A little girl started to cry.

"There are more to choose from," Lily comforted her, shooting Nanea a look of desperation. "Explain faster."

Nanea hurried through the first step.

"He kicked me!" A red-headed girl pointed at Lewis. Bernice made a face.

"Let's keep our hands and our feet to ourselves." Nanea wiped perspiration off her forehead. "Now choose two smaller scraps for ears," she instructed. That step happened without too much fuss. "Next, we'll glue the ears to the head."

Two little girls instantly got stuck together and started crying. Another little girl started crying because the first two girls were crying.

Nanea clapped her hands over her ears. *Why, oh why, did I give up a fishing trip for this?* she wondered.

"I've got glue in my hair," complained a boy in a blue-and-white checkered *palaka* shirt.

Nanea smiled weakly. "Donna, can you help him?"

Somehow, Donna ended up with glue in her hair, too. And Lewis was sprinkling glitter everywhere. Two brothers at the far end of the table were throwing buttons at each other. One of them was crying. Nanea felt like crying herself.

Nanea bent to comfort the crying brother, and her pouch slipped out from under the collar of her dress.

"What's that?" Patricia asked.

"Oh, a pouch I made for my ID card," Nanea answered.

Patricia looked at it closely. "This might make a better project for these little guys. Simpler than stuffed animals. *And* it would be something useful."

"Great idea!" Donna yanked at the glue in her hair.

"Tell us what to do," Debby said.

"First thing is to get rid of the glue and glitter!" Nanea said. Then she began snapping off commands like a general, and the commotion calmed to a quiet roar. "Who wants to make a pouch?" she asked. "You can use it for coins or treasures or an ID card if you have one." Once she showed the little kids what they were going to make, they started to pay attention.

"I want to make one for my big brother, too," Lewis said, his hair sparkling with glitter.

"Only if you stop kicking," Nanea said.

"Okay." Lewis smiled.

Bernice led the kids in a game of Simon Says, while Nanea showed her friends how to make the drawstring pouch. Soon everyone was working together. The kids picked the fabrics and decorations, and the girls did the stitching. When the mothers finished their class and came to collect their children, there were no more tears in the room.

"What great babysitters you are," Lewis's mother said when she picked him up.

Nanea grinned. They were definitely essential.

Once their charges were gone, all the girls wanted to make pouches for themselves. "Look at this!" Donna modeled hers. "It's niftier than a bracelet."

Nanea couldn't stop smiling as she gathered the glue- and glitter-smeared newspaper from the tables.

"How did it go?" Mom asked.

"It was fine at the *end*." Nanea told Mom the whole story. "I had no idea it would take so much work."

Mom laughed. "It was a big project. The important thing is that you didn't give up." She cocked her head as she looked at Nanea. "You really are growing up! You were such a big help today."

"I hope we can help again," Nanea said, thinking,

anything to keep Donna in Honolulu.

"I'm sure you'll have plenty of chances. Say, it seems like what you did today could count toward that Helping Hands contest," Mom said. "You definitely helped the community."

"I guess so," Nanea shrugged. "But the deadline for the contest was yesterday."

"Oh, honey. You missed it!" Mom said sadly. "I'm sorry. I should have made a note on the calendar."

"It's okay," Nanea said. And it was. She didn't care much about winning something for herself anymore. Now that she had dipped her paddle in, Nanea wanted to keep helping others. Like Donna. If her plan worked, Donna would get to stay.

DIPPING HER PADDLE

ail from the mainland!" Mom exclaimed after breakfast. "Letters from Grandmom and Grandpop all around." She handed envelopes to Nanea, Mary Lou, and David.

David read from his. "Grandpop says their hired man has enlisted." He sighed. "Three more of my friends from McKinley High School signed up this week. I wish I was already eighteen."

Nanea looked at the kitchen calendar. Today was January twentieth. It was less than six months until David's eighteenth birthday. Would he wake up on June fifth and enlist?

"Your work shirt is ironed," Mom said, changing the subject.

David grabbed his shirt and kissed Mom good-bye. "Thanks. See you all tonight," he said.

After David left, Mom was very quiet. Nanea could
see the little worry lines on her forehead. David-worry
lines. Nanea wanted to say something, but Donna
appeared at the back door.

"We're heading to Lily's," Nanea called.

"Don't forget your gas mask!" reminded Mary Lou.

Nanea groaned. "Do I have to take it?"

"Yes," Mom said. "It's the rule."

The military was worried that the Japanese would
return and release poisonous gas, so everyone in
Hawaii was required to carry a mask. Everywhere. All
the time. Even kids.

When the masks had first been issued, Nanea had
felt like a real soldier for the war effort. But the masks
were as heavy as bowling balls. And hot! Luckily,
there'd only been one gas drill so far.

Nanea shifted her mask in her arms this way and
that as she and Donna walked down the block.

"These things are so heavy," Nanea grumbled.

"And hard to hang on to." Donna struggled with
hers as well.

Nanea shook her head. "It looks like you're wres-
tling with a sea monster!"

"And losing!" Donna blew a big bubble, snapping it back in her mouth.

"You better not do that with your mask on," Nanea warned.

"Good advice." Donna grinned. "What would I do without you?"

When they got to Lily's, they added their gas masks to the pile in the front hall.

Lily's living room was full. All the girls who had helped the Three Kittens with the babysitting adventure were there. The Red Cross was planning to have more first aid classes and wanted the group to babysit again. Nanea had gotten everyone together to plan some more activities and games to do with the little kids. But she also wanted to talk to her friends about doing other service projects. There had to be more ways to show that Donna was essential and needed to stay in Honolulu.

"We could do a scrap drive," Donna suggested. "Uncle Sam needs metal and rubber and paper to make war equipment."

Lily giggled. "Gene's scout troop collected rubber, and some lady gave them three old girdles!"

All the girls laughed. "Even underwear can help the war effort," Nanea said. Then she cleared her throat to share an idea. "Every day the paper prints notices asking people to donate blood," she said.

"Blood?" Lily paled.

Nanea fished a newspaper photograph from her pocket and passed it around. "Even Duke Kahanamoku has donated." The famous surfer was now Honolulu's sheriff.

"Aren't we too young to donate blood?" Lily asked, her voice shaking.

"Yes, we are," Nanea answered. "But we're not too young to collect bottles."

Lily looked relieved.

"After the attack, my brother delivered bottles of blood from the Red Cross to the hospital," Nanea explained. "As fast as he delivered them, the hospital needed more. They still need blood. And guess what?" She leaned forward. "There's a bottle shortage." She showed them the other articles she'd clipped from the paper, all about the Red Cross pleading for bottles. "They're essential," she said, smiling at Donna. "So I think that's what we should collect."

"Different!" Donna exclaimed.

"We'd be the first," said Judy.

"Let's do it!" Lily and Makana clapped their hands.

The girls' voices buzzed as they started making plans. "This will be the biggest drive on the island," Lily predicted.

Nanea was proud to have thought of it.

The next morning, Nanea got up and dressed quietly while Mary Lou snored away.

"My goodness," Mom said when Nanea joined her in the kitchen. "Who's this early bird?"

"The bottle bird," Nanea answered.

Mom set two empty juice bottles on the counter. "I saved these to start you off."

"Thanks!" Nanea polished off her papaya and eggs. "Got to go!"

Gas mask in hand, she ran to the meeting spot on the corner, Mele loping along behind. Donna was already there. A moment later, Lily clattered down the street pulling Tommy's red wagon.

"Our first donations!" Nanea proudly placed

Mom's bottles in the wagon.

Mrs. Nicholson smiled when she opened her door. "My favorite neighbors," she said. Then she saw their wagon. "I'm sorry. I donated newspapers last week."

"Oh, this isn't a paper drive," Nanea said. "It's for bottles."

"Bottles? Well, that's a horse of a different color." Mrs. Nicholson disappeared into her bungalow and returned with two more bottles. "Good luck!"

Donna knocked at the next house.

"I'm all out of scrap metal," Mr. Brown shook his head.

"But we're collecting bottles!" Donna said quickly.

Mr. Brown scratched his nose. "Well, I believe I have a spare." And he did.

The third house was Mrs. Lin's. She added three more to their collection. And, thanks to her, word began to spread. By lunchtime, the red wagon was full.

"We should empty this so the bottles don't break," Nanea suggested.

Donna rubbed her middle. "I'm starved."

They emptied the wagon at Nanea's house, carefully packing the bottles into boxes from Pono's

Market. Then they devoured the fried bologna sandwiches Mom whipped up.

The Kittens went out three more times after lunch, returning with a full wagon each time. They brought back a last load as David arrived home from work.

"What's going on here?" he asked.

Nanea filled him in.

"And you thought of that?" He ruffled Nanea's hair. "That blood really saves lives." David looked thoughtful. "Do you remember me telling you about Stan?"

Nanea nodded. "That's what gave me the idea. You were my inspiration."

David looked surprised. "And I am inspired to help you deliver these bottles. Let's get them loaded into my trunk."

The girls had collected so many bottles that they didn't all fit into David's car. "That's okay," David said. "We have time for a couple of trips before curfew. Are you lovely ladies coming along?"

"Yes!" Nanea answered for the other Kittens, who made quick calls to their mothers for permission.

As the car jostled down the road, Nanea hollered

to David, "For once I can't hear the engine. The bottles are too loud!"

"Are you making fun of my car?" David poked her in the side.

Nanea laughed.

At the Red Cross building, David pulled around to the back and honked his horn. Three Red Cross ladies opened the loading dock doors. One wore a hat, and one wore glasses. The third lady had blue-gray hair.

"Oh, my!" the hat lady exclaimed when David popped the trunk.

"You don't know how precious this cargo is," the glasses lady said.

"More precious than diamonds," the blue-hair lady added. "We've had such a bottle shortage. You girls are the answer to our prayers!"

"Well, this is only the first load," Nanea said.

"And the first day!" Donna added.

"I think I might cry." The hat lady pulled out a handkerchief.

The blue-hair lady held up her hand. "Cry later," she said. "Now, we need to unload this treasure!"

When the last bottle had been carried inside and

placed in big storage bins, the Red Cross ladies told the girls that the next step would be sterilizing. "Then they'll be filled and put to use," the blue-hair lady explained.

"We'll be back with more!" Nanea promised as they waved good-bye.

"They sure were impressed," David said as he started the car. "Great job, little Monkey."

"Great job, Kittens, you mean." But Nanea felt proud enough to burst. She'd finally found a way to do something big for the island *and* show Uncle Sam that girls like Donna were essential.

Talking Story

CHAPTER 20

A car horn sounded out front. "Mrs. Hill is here!" Nanea called.

"We're ready." Mary Lou and Iris picked up their beach bags and followed Nanea outside.

Donna had cooked up a plan for a picnic at Waikiki Beach to celebrate their hard work with the bottle drive. "Plus school's starting again in just nine short days," Donna had explained when she'd suggested the outing. She'd looked sad. Donna wasn't as crazy about school as Nanea was.

Nanea, on the other hand, couldn't wait. She had circled the first day of school, February 2, on her calendar. Finally, something would be back to normal. She was eager to see Miss Smith again, even if they wouldn't be in the same classroom next to the library.

Mrs. Hill dropped the Kittens and their chaper-
ones near the Royal Hawaiian Hotel. "Have fun!" She
waved as she drove away.

"Last one to the beach is a rotten egg!" Donna took
off running, with Lily quickly catching up. Mary Lou
and Iris strolled behind them, carrying the ice chest.

Nanea stood for a moment looking at the barbed
wire, which had been stretched across the beach right
after the Pearl Harbor attack. There were a few spots
where people could pass through to get to the water.
The wire was supposed to keep them safe if there was
an enemy invasion, but the giant spools with their
sharp edges made Nanea feel uneasy.

"Come on, slowpoke!" Donna called back to Nanea.
She and Lily had already ducked through the opening
in the wire and were heading toward the surf.

"Meow!" added Lily.

Nanea slipped through the hole in the barbed wire
and ran to meet her friends. They spent the day playing
in the ocean, doing cartwheels in the sand, and pre-
tending to be spies as they watched Mary Lou and Iris
watch the surfers.

After lunch, Donna offered to treat them to shave

ice. As they strolled across the sand, Nanea said, "I have an idea. Let's order Kitten shave ice."

"What's that?" Donna asked.

"You'll see." Nanea ordered for all of them.

"A rainbow!" the shave ice man said, drizzling lemon, orange, and strawberry syrups over three cups of shave ice.

"They're delicious!" Donna said. Her lips were already pink.

"And they include each of our favorite flavors," Lily added.

After the shave ice, the girls ran to the ocean to wash off the sticky syrup. The water swirled around Nanea's ankles, filling the footprints she'd made. She shaded her eyes and studied the sun. It was nearly time to leave. This day was like her footprints—filled up in a quick moment. She wasn't ready for it to end.

"Let's do a pinky swear," Donna said suddenly.

"About what?" asked Lily.

"That you won't forget me." Donna drew a circle in the sand with her toe.

Nanea shook her head. "Are you still worried about being sent away?"

Donna nodded slowly. "I heard Mom and Dad whispering about it last night."

"You are *not* leaving," Nanea insisted. She was confident about her plan to prove that Donna was essential. "Besides, we could never forget you."

Lily nodded. The girls stepped together, connected in a tight circle by their touching pinkies. "We'll always be the Three Kittens," Lily said.

Together they said, "We swear!"

Donna glanced at her wristwatch. A sad look passed over her face. "It's time to go meet Mom," she said.

As Mary Lou and Iris helped the girls gather up their things, Donna pulled out her camera. "Mary Lou, will you take a picture of us?" she asked.

"That's the first photo you've wanted to take today," Lily pointed out.

Donna wrapped her arms around each of her friends. "You don't always need a picture to remember what matters."

On Monday, Nanea found Mom on the telephone. That wasn't unusual. She was often on the phone these days with Red Cross business. But this time Nanea overheard her own name.

"I'm certain that could be arranged," Mom nodded. "Yes, that's fine. I'll tell her. Thank you, Miss Allen." Mom hung up. "That was Gwenfread Allen, a reporter at the *Star-Bulletin*, calling about the bottle drive. She wants to interview you and have a picture taken for the newspaper." Mom brushed some hair out of Nanea's face. "I am so proud of you!"

Nanea felt proud, too.

"Miss Allen asked that you bring the other girls along. Two o'clock this Thursday, January 29, at the Red Cross Center."

Nanea raced to Lily's house with a huge smile on her face.

"What's going on?" Lily asked as Nanea pulled her off the front porch.

All Nanea would say was, "I'll tell you at Donna's."

Nanea and Lily were out of breath by the time they knocked on the Hills' front door.

No one came. Nanea knocked again. Finally, Mrs. Hill answered.

"Oh, girls," she said. Her voice was so sad. "You

are just the medicine Donna needs." Mrs. Hill stepped aside so Nanea and Lily could come in, and Nanea saw that the living room was full of cardboard boxes. One was packed with pots and pans, one with towels, and several with clothes.

"What are all these boxes?" Nanea asked.

Mrs. Hill sighed. "We got some difficult news today."

Nanea's heart stopped.

Mrs. Hill picked up a blanket, folding it into a neat square. "We have to leave Honolulu. Leave Oahu." She placed the blanket in one of the boxes. "We're shipping out with the other nonessentials—"

"No!" Nanea cried. Not after all she had done to show that Donna was essential! Nanea grabbed Lily's hand and ran to Donna's room.

Donna was slumped on the floor, a box of tissues in her lap. "I told you," she said. "I told you it would happen." Tears dripped down her face.

Nanea fought tears of her own. Donna was essential. What about helping Auntie Rose with the camouflage nets, and the babysitting, and collecting all those bottles?

"I thought it was a dumb old rumor," Lily said.

"But it's not." Donna sniffled. "It's not." She grabbed a handful of tissues. Lily and Nanea grabbed some, too. The girls sat together, sniffling. Finally, Nanea had to ask the horrible question. "When do you have to leave?"

"We don't know for sure," Donna whispered. "They'll only give us twenty-four hours notice."

Nanea's heart sank like a stone tossed into the surf.

"One day?" Lily asked in a small voice.

Nanea thought about the news she had planned to share. She told Donna and Lily about the photograph for the newspaper. "It's on Thursday," she said.

"Maybe I'll still be here," Donna said hopefully.

Nanea closed her eyes. *Donna has to be here for the photo*, she told herself. *She just has to.*

When Nanea got home, Papa was reading the paper in the living room. "That's the biggest storm cloud I've ever seen on your face," he said. He put the newspaper down. "What's up?"

Nanea sat on the sofa next to him, her elbows on

her knees, chin in her hands. "Donna and Mrs. Hill have to leave, but they don't know when," she said softly. "It could even be tomorrow!"

Papa shook his head. "Because of that order about nonessential personnel," he said.

Nanea nodded. "But Papa, Donna *is* essential! I came up with a plan to prove it." She described to him everything that they had done. "It's not fair." Nanea started to cry.

Papa gave Nanea his handkerchief. "You're right. It's not fair. You have done so much to help the war effort. So has Donna. You did all the right things." He sighed. "But, honey, no amount of good deeds could've kept Donna here. The Army is trying to keep the island safe. They've made this decision for the good of all."

The decision didn't feel very good to Nanea.

"I know I've been gone a lot, but I've noticed a change in you," Papa put his arm around Nanea's shoulder. "I see you thinking first, and then acting wisely. And you've certainly made sacrifices. Like choosing to babysit instead of going fishing."

Nanea sniffled and wiped her eyes.

Papa squeezed her two times. Buddies forever.

"You're not the baby of the family anymore," he said.

Just a few weeks ago, those words would have made Nanea so happy. But now she understood why Mom had told her not to be in a hurry to grow up. There was no going back.

"Over here, girls!" The photographer waved his hand above his head. "Look at me. One more shot."

Nanea adjusted the orchid lei around her neck. The Red Cross ladies had them made for all the girls so they'd look festive in the photo. Nanea reached over to straighten Donna's lei, relieved that she and her mother hadn't gotten the call yet. "There," Nanea said.

Donna blew a bubble. "Thanks, pal! What would I do without you?"

Nanea smiled bravely, but inside she wondered, *What am I going to do without you?*

"Okay, that's a wrap." The photographer started to put his equipment away. "Unless you need anything else, Gwen."

Miss Allen shook her head. She looked more like a movie star than a reporter. She wore her dark hair swept back into a fancy chignon style. A pearl necklace encircled her long, elegant neck. She led Nanea away from her friends to a quiet corner of the room for the interview. "What inspired you to start this bottle drive?" Miss Allen asked, her pencil poised over a slim notepad.

Nanea told her about David's experience at the hospital in the days after the attack. She told Miss Allen how her hula school danced at the USO to cheer up soldiers and about her friends babysitting during the Red Cross first aid class. "But I wanted to do something different, something more, to help."

"You and your friends have collected fifteen hundred bottles so far. That will help a lot of people." Miss Allen looked up from her notepad and smiled. "I bet you will inspire even more people to pitch in. I guess it's true when they say 'a little child shall lead them.'"

Nanea smiled weakly and nodded.

Miss Allen studied Nanea's face. "You don't look very happy about that."

"Oh, I am," Nanea replied. "Really."

Miss Allen waited with a patient expression.

"I'm sad about something else," Nanea confessed.

"My friend has to leave Hawaii." Nanea couldn't stop the tear from trickling down her face. "The government says she's nonessential. But she's not non-essential to me!"

Miss Allen wrote something on her notepad. "So much has changed since December seventh," she said. "For everyone. But I think this war has been toughest on you kids. I'm sorry."

Nanea nodded, wiping her cheek.

"Thank you for trusting me with your story," Miss Allen said. She stood up and shook Nanea's hand.

Nanea walked back over to Donna and Lily. For a moment, no one said anything, and then Donna reached into her pocket.

"Anyone want a piece of gum?" she asked.

"I do!" Lily held out her hand.

Nanea sighed. "Me, too."

ALOHAS AT THE DOCK

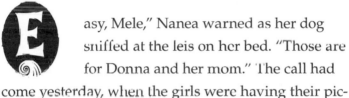

asy, Mele," Nanea warned as her dog sniffed at the leis on her bed. "Those are for Donna and her mom." The call had come yesterday, when the girls were having their picture taken. Donna and her mom were leaving today.

Mele tucked her muzzle between her front paws, her brown eyes full of sadness.

David leaned into the room and tapped the door frame. "This war won't last forever, you know."

Nanea pressed her face into the ruff of fur at Mele's neck, afraid she'd start blubbering. "This dumb war is taking away everything good," she mumbled.

"You have every right to be sad, Monkey. And mad."

Nanea peeked at him. "I do?"

"Oh, yeah." David spread his arms wide. "This

whole big wide world deserves the stink eye from my baby sis."

Nanea ducked her face. "You're making fun of me."

"No, I'm not." David's face was serious. "Go ahead," he encouraged. "Big-time stink eye." He did it himself, making it look as if he was smelling a pile of rotting fish.

She wrinkled her nose halfheartedly.

David shook his head. "Come on, Monkey. I know you can do better than that!"

Nanea squinted and scowled, making the stinkiest stink eye she could. "Grrr!" David laughed, and then Nanea did, too. "It does help a little," she admitted.

Papa appeared in the doorway. "We need to leave," he said gently. The trunk of Papa's car was loaded with some of the Hills' belongings to deliver to the ship.

"I'm coming." Nanea carefully picked up each of the four leis she'd made.

"Auntie Rose would be proud of these," Papa said. "They're beautiful!"

"They are full of aloha," Nanea said softly. "And Auntie says that's what counts."

On the porch, Nanea put on her rubber slippers.

"Ready?" Mom asked, pulling on her good hat.

"Well, the leis are ready," Nanea answered. "But I'm not." Tears stung her eyes again.

Mom brought her close for a hug. "I know this is tough for you." She kissed Nanea's forehead. "But it takes more than an ocean to separate good friends."

Nanea climbed in the backseat and Papa drove up the block, stopping in front of the Sudas' house. Lily came running out, carrying a package, and slid into the back with Nanea.

"Oh, those are beautiful," Lily said, admiring the leis in Nanea's lap.

"That's beautiful, too." The box Lily held was exquisitely wrapped in pink paper. With Japanese gift-giving, the outside of a present was almost more important than the inside.

Lily patted her package. "I made a frame out of Popsicle sticks and painted island flowers—jasmine and hibiscus and wild ginger—all around the edges." She pantomimed using a paintbrush. "I thought she could use it for the photo your dad took of the three of us last night."

Nanea nodded. Their families had gathered for one

last meal with the Hills. When Papa took the picture, Nanea had forced a smile. She didn't want to feel too sad when she looked at the snapshot later.

Nanea glanced out the window as they drove past their school. Workmen pounded wood over the hole in the second-floor roof. "Do you think it'll be ready for us by Monday?"

"It's going to be so different," Lily said. "No Donna. And no Room 204."

Miss Smith's magical classroom had been destroyed. Her students would be doubling up in another room. Would it have a shiny red pencil sharpener? Or a spinning globe? Nanea scolded herself. Those were only things. What mattered most about the new classroom was that Miss Smith would be there. Miss Smith would know just what to say and do to keep Nanea from missing Donna.

Lily poked her in the side. "There's the Aloha Tower."

That meant they were almost to the pier.

Once, boat departures meant lei sellers and hula dancers and the Royal Hawaiian band. Now, they meant soldiers guarding the dock and sad good-byes.

Lily slid out of the car and smoothed her skirt. "I hope we can find Donna and her parents."

Crowds of people pushed past them, trying to get as close as they could to the fences around the dock. Nanea lost her balance in the wake of a rushing family.

"We'll never find them," Lily said.

"We have to!" Nanea insisted. Something pink caught her attention. A bubble! "There!" She dragged Lily along. "Donna! Donna!" she called.

The Three Kittens ran to one another while the adults scurried to keep up.

"We were scared we wouldn't find you," Lily said.

"I wouldn't have gotten on the ship without a good-bye." Donna stamped her foot. "No matter what the captain said!"

Seeing Donna in her best dress with socks and black patent Mary Janes made Nanea too shy to speak for a moment. Then Donna snapped her gum, breaking the awkwardness. Underneath the fancy clothes was still the same old Donna.

Lily presented her gift. "This is so you never forget us." Her voice was full of emotion. "You can open it on the ship."

"These are for you, too." Nanea slipped one lei over Donna's head, and Mrs. Hill bent down to accept hers.

"The heavenly smell of the islands." Mrs. Hill's words were happy, but her face was sad. "Thank you." She hugged both girls, and then stepped away with Mr. Hill to talk to Nanea's parents.

Donna looked over at her father. "I don't know when I'll get to see my dad again," she said.

Lily grabbed her hand. "It really hurts to have a puka in your family. I know. But it's not forever."

Donna sniffled. "I'm just worried about him."

"We'll take care of him," Lily assured Donna.

Nanea agreed. "We'll invite him to supper. He is part of our 'ohana."

Donna gave a wobbly smile. "You two are the best. Thank you."

"Don't forget these," Nanea said. She gave Donna the two remaining leis.

"Mom and I will throw them overboard," Donna promised. "So that we'll come back."

The boat horn blasted three times. "Time to go aboard," called Mrs. Hill.

The three best friends couldn't bear to look at

one another. Then Nanea put out her pinky. Lily and Donna stuck theirs out, too.

"Kittens forever!" Nanea said.

"Pinky swear," they all said in unison.

Though Nanea had promised herself she wouldn't cry, the tears that had been building up all morning broke through. Matching tear trails trickled down her friends' faces.

Mr. Hill knelt down and gave Donna a long, long hug. Then he stood up and pulled out his handkerchief.

"Come on, dear." Mrs. Hill took Donna's hand. She started for the line of soldiers who were guarding the entrance to the docks. No one, not even Mr. Hill, could go any farther unless they had a ticket to board.

"We'll wave till the ship is out of sight!" Lily called.

"Until our arms fall off," Nanea shouted.

Donna and her mother climbed the steps to the pier and disappeared. Nanea and Lily waited, peering through the fencing. They searched the top deck of the ship, where Donna said she would be.

"There she is!" Nanea finally called.

"She's throwing her lei overboard," Lily added.

Donna's lei drifted down from the ship's rail and

landed with a small splash in the water. It bobbed along with the currents. The white plumeria shimmered like pearls on the waves.

Nanea watched as the lei floated back to shore, longing with her whole heart for the day that Donna, too, would return to their beautiful island.

INSIDE Nanea's World

Hawaii is located in the Pacific Ocean, more than 2,000 miles west of the continental United States. Although the islands were a U.S. territory in 1941, many mainland Americans did not know where Hawaii was. That all changed on Sunday, December 7, when the Japanese attacked the Pearl Harbor naval base near Honolulu on the island of Oahu. Suddenly, everyone knew where Hawaii was, and they knew that America was at war.

World War Two changed life for all Americans, but the changes were especially dramatic for the residents of Hawaii. Schools were closed immediately. The beaches were lined with barbed wire. Nearly half the parks were taken over by the military for storage. The docks, once open to everyone for festive Boat Day celebrations, were now off-limits. Long-distance phone calls were monitored, and mail was *censored*, which meant it was read, and sometimes altered, before it was delivered.

Living in Hawaii meant following new rules. No one could be outside after curfew unless they had a special pass. "If we went visiting at someone's house for dinner," one resident remembers, "we would take our pajamas and stay all night." Blackouts were strictly enforced from 6:00 p.m. to 6:00 a.m. For people like Nanea, it was difficult to endure long evenings inside with all the windows and doors closed. Without the cool island breezes, homes became horribly hot.

These changes were part of *martial law,* which was declared on December 7. Hawaii was the only place in the country where the law was enforced. It went into effect in part because of the large population of people of Japanese descent. In 1941, they were the largest ethnic group in Hawaii and made up nearly 35 percent of the population. Like the Sudas, many Japanese families sent their children to Japanese schools, clubs, or religious organizations to maintain ties to their country's language and customs. After the attack on Pearl Harbor, military leaders were suspicious of Japanese residents. Could they be trusted as Americans, or would they be loyal to Japan? Martial law allowed the military to closely monitor and control all civilians.

Nanea didn't understand how anyone could mistrust their neighbors. Hawaiian culture is based on the spirit of *aloha*—the idea that everyone is connected to one another, and that joys and sorrows are shared. Like many islanders, Nanea was eager to help the war effort so that life could get back to normal.

There were plenty of ways children helped. Girls and boys volunteered in hospitals, first-aid stations, and offices. They cooked, served food, and washed dishes for aid workers and people in evacuation centers. They ran errands, delivered supplies, became junior nurses' aides, and looked after children. Many kids took on grown-up responsibilities. Across the islands, people of all ages showed their patriotism with true aloha spirit.

GLOSSARY of Hawaiian Words

ae *(AYE)*—yes, agreement

'ahi *(AH-hee)*—a large tuna fish

aloha *(ah-LO-hah)*—hello, good-bye, love, compassion

'eke hula *(EH-kay HOO-la)*—a bag or basket used to carry hula implements and costumes

haole *(HOW-lay)*—a foreigner, usually a white person

hapa *(HAH-pah)*—a part or portion, half

haumana *(how-MAH-nah)*—student

holoku *(ho-loh-KOO)*—a floor-length formal gown with a train

ho'okipa *(ho-oh-KEE-pah)*—hospitality, to show hospitality

imu *(EE-moo)*—a large covered pit where food is baked by hot stones

ipu *(EE-poo)*—gourd drum

kala'au *(KAH-lah-OW)*—a pair of hardwood sticks used as hula instruments

kalua *(kah-LOO-ah)*—to bake in an underground oven

keiki *(KAY-kee)*—child

kokua *(KOH-KOO-ah)*—assistance, a good deed, to help

komo mai *(KOH-mo MY)*—a greeting of welcome

kumu hula *(KOO-moo HOO-lah)*—hula teacher

lanai *(LAH-nye)*—covered porch

lei *(LAY)*—a wreath of flowers, feathers, or shells worn around the neck or head

lei po'o *(LAY POH-oh)*—a wreath of flowers, feathers, or shells worn on the head

mahalo *(mah-HAH-loh)*—thank you

makaukau *(MAH-kow-KOW)*—ready, prepared

mele *(MEH-leh)*—song

Mele Kalikimake *(MEH-leh kah-lee-kee-MAH-kah)*—Merry Christmas

menehune *(meh-nah-HOO-neh)*—a legendary race of small people who worked through the night

mu'umu'u *(MOO-ooh MOO-ooh)*—a long, loose-fitting dress without a train, usually made from brightly colored or patterned fabric

nani *(NAH-nee)*—beautiful

'ohana *(oh-HAH-nuh)*—family

'ono *(OH-no)*—tasty, delicious

palaka *(pah-LAH-kah)*—a checker-patterned cloth used to make work shirts and casual clothes

poi *(POY)*—a starchy pudding made from pounded taro root. A *poi dog* is a mixed-breed dog, named for a now-extinct breed that was fed poi.

pu'ili *(pooh-EE-lee)*—bamboo sticks used as hula instruments

puka *(POO-kah)*—hole. Puka shells have holes in the center.

taro *(TAIR-oh)*—a tropical plant with a starchy, edible root

tutu *(TOO-too)*—grandparent, usually grandmother

tutu kane *(TOO-too KAH-nay)*—grandfather

Read more of NANEA'S stories,
available from booksellers and at *americangirl.com*

❀ *Classics* ❀
Nanea's classic series in two volumes:

Volume 1:
Growing Up with Aloha
Nanea may be the youngest in her family, but she *knows* she's ready for more responsibility. When Japan attacks Pearl Harbor and America goes to war, Nanea is faced with grown-up chores and choices.

Volume 2:
Hula for the Home Front
The war has changed everything in Nanea's world. She's trying to "do her part," but it's not easy to make so many sacrifices. Hula, and a surprising dance partner, help Nanea hold on to her aloha spirit. .

❀ *Journey in Time* ❀
Travel back in time—and spend a few days with Nanea!

Prints in the Sand
Step into Nanea's world of Hawaii during World War Two. Learn how to dance a hula. Help a lost dog. Work in a Victory Garden, or send secret messages for the war effort. Choose your own path through this multiple-ending story.

❀ A Sneak Peek at ❀

Hula
for the
Home Front

A Nanea Classic

Volume 2

Nanea's adventures continue in the
second volume of her classic stories.

anea and Lily crossed the street and entered the school building. Normally, they would've hurried up the worn wooden stairs to their classroom. But the stairs were blocked by yellow ropes tied between the bannisters. Workers were still repairing the library and classrooms that had been damaged in the December 7th fire.

The girls made their way to a smaller classroom on the first floor and squeezed through the aisle to take the same seats they'd had in their old classroom near the windows. They hung the straps of their gas masks from the backs of their chairs.

More kids wandered in, including a girl Nanea hadn't seen before. Finally, Miss Smith sailed into the classroom. "Good morning, scholars," she said.

The cares and worries of the past months slipped off Nanea's shoulders. Miss Smith was like Superman, swooping in to save them all from the troubles of the world.

Miss Smith asked Lily to lead the flag salute. Then she took attendance. The new girl answered, "here," when Miss Smith called out "Dixie Moreno."

"Dixie, we're so glad you've joined our class,"

Miss Smith said. "Would you like to tell us a bit about yourself?"

Dixie had a short brown pageboy haircut and a slightly crooked smile. She stood up confidently at her desk. "I've moved here from Maui because my dad has a new job at Wheeler Airfield. I love tap dancing, and when I'm older I'm getting three dogs." She smiled. "I can't have any now because my dad's allergic." She sat down.

"Welcome, Dixie," Miss Smith said. "I think you'll find we're a friendly crew."

Nanea didn't feel completely friendly about Dixie, who was sitting where Donna's seat should be. But Nanea felt badly that Dixie wanted a dog and couldn't have one.

"Now, before we begin our lessons I want to assign classroom jobs." As Miss Smith called students' names, she had each person come forward to get a small cardboard tent to place on his or her desk. The tents said what job the student had been assigned. Nanea waited patiently for her name to be called. Miss Smith always called Nanea her "right-hand girl." Nanea couldn't wait to see what job she would get.

One by one the tents disappeared from Miss
Smith's desk. Then she picked up the last tent. "The
War Stamps monitor will be in charge of the weekly
War Stamps sale," Miss Smith explained. "Every stamp
helps the war effort, so this job is very important."

Now Nanea knew why Miss Smith hadn't called her
name yet. She was saving the biggest job for her right-
hand girl.

Miss Smith smiled. "I am going to assign this to . . ."

Nanea sat up nice and tall.

"Dixie Moreno," Miss Smith said, beaming at the
new girl.

"I'll do my very best," Dixie said.

A little crab of jealousy pinched at Nanea. Why
would Miss Smith give such a big job to the new kid?
Someone who didn't even know everyone's names?
Someone who liked tap dancing? It wasn't fair.

About the Author

KIRBY LARSON is the author of several novels, including the Newbery Honor book *Hattie Big Sky*, and *Dash*, winner of the Scott O'Dell Award for Historical Fiction. With her friend Mary Nethery, she has written two award-winning picture books. She lives in Kenmore, Washington, with her husband and Winston the wonder dog. In her free time, she hunts for beach glass and tidbits from history that she can turn into stories for young readers. Visit Kirby at www.kirbylarson.com.

Advisory Board

*American Girl extends its deepest appreciation
to the advisory board that authenticated Nanea's stories.*

Linda Arthur Bradley

Professor of Apparel, Merchandising, Design, and Textiles,
Washington State University, and author of *Aloha Attire*
(Schiffer Publishing, 2000)

DeSoto Brown

Hawaii native, Collection Manager, Archives, Bishop Museum,
Honolulu, and author of *Hawaii Goes to War: Life in Hawaii from
Pearl Harbor to Peace* (Editions Ltd, 1989)

Patricia Lei Murray

Hawaii native, hula and quilting expert, and author of *Hawaiian
Quilt Inspirations* (Mutual Publishing, 2003) and *Cherished Hawaiian
Quilts* (Mutual Publishing, 2015)

Dorinda Makanaonalani Nicholson

Hawaii native, hula expert, eyewitness to the bombing of Pearl
Harbor, and author of *Pearl Harbor Child: A Child's View of Pearl
Harbor—From Attack to Peace* (Woodson House Printing, 2001)

Marvin Puakea Nogelmeier

Professor, Kawaihuelani Center for Hawaiian Language,
University of Hawaii at Manoa, and author of *Mai Pa'a I Ka Leo:
Historical Voices in Hawaiian Primary Materials, Looking Forward
and Listening Back* (Bishop Museum Press, 2010)